RETURN TO SAIGON

It was getting dark and there were a few taxis out front letting off passengers. Comrad Kim was saying something; I was looking for the Chinaman. Suddenly an engine roared and a taxi not in the line came tearing down the street with its high beams on. It swerved over toward us and then I saw the Chinaman sticking an M-16 out through the back window.

"Get down!" I yelled at Kim, shoving her to one side. The M-16 rattled bullets at us. People behind us were cut down by the blast and Kim wa pulling an automatic pistol from her shoulder bag when a lurching body hit her and knocked her down. The automatic went skittering on the concrete and I dived for it while the taxi began to back up so the Chinaman could get a better shot at us. I could see the Chinaman's face over the top of the rifle. I gave the Chinaman and the taxi most of the clip. He took some bullets in the face and the M-16 fell out the window. I fired at the taxi. It swerved sideways and was struck by a van that tried to get out of its way. The collision killed the motor, then the driver jumped out bloody-faced and staggering and ran into the parking lot.

I pulled Kim to her feet. People were running in and out of the hotel; a police jeep with two men in it pulled up with a screech of tires. They jumped out and menaced everyone with their submachine guns. Dead and wounded were on the steps and the sidewalk, and there was a lot of blood.

Cover Posed by Professional Model

Also in the SOLDIER OF FORTUNE series:

YELLOW RAIN
GREEN HELL
MORO
KALAHARI

SOLDIER OF FORTUNE
GOLDEN TRIANGLE

Peter McCurtin

LEISURE BOOKS  NEW YORK CITY

A LEISURE BOOK

Published by

Dorchester Publishing Co., Inc.
6 East 39th Street
New York, NY 10016

Printed in the United States of America

ONE

NOT ALL Mafia mobsters have "dese," "dems," and "dose" accents. They don't all wear dark suits and ice cream ties and half-pound cufflinks. Not all have Bimini tans and faces like unsuccessful middleweights. Recently, I think, a lot of them have been reading that book *How to Dress for Success*, which goes far beyond cautioning the reader not to wear brown shoes with a blue suit.

The elderly guy who came to see me after a brief telephone call would never be taken for an investment banker. If challenged to guess his occupation, you might put him down as the owner of a chain of laundromats, a taxi-fleet operator, a retired undertaker. You might do that, but I wouldn't. I know a mobster when I see one, even when he walks around without a bodyguard.

My name is Jim Rainey and I'm a mercenary—a soldier of fortune, if you want to use the more romantic term—and I had just come back from an overseas job and was laying over in New York, drinking a little, taking a few broads to Broadway shows and later to bed. I come from Beaumont, Texas, and still own the

5

old house on the river where I grew up. After New York got to be too much, and it doesn't take long, I thought I would go back there for a while.

It was a good hotel and the desk called and said Mr. Joseph Albergo wanted to come up.

"Okay," I said.

I knew the name from the newspapers and the TV news. Two years before the Feds had prosecuted him for racketeering, a new Government dodge that has replaced persecution by the IRS, but they hadn't been able to send him away. Since then, nothing much had been heard of him. A mild-mannered goombah in the Frank Costello mold, he didn't even have a nickname, though facetious newspapermen tried to hang one on him when they had nothing better to do.

Because he was a very small man, almost tiny, they tried out Joe the Jockey, Joe the Runt, Little Joe, Half Pint, and Short Pants. None of them caught on; Joe Albergo resisted their best efforts to give him "color."

He buzzed and I let him in, a hammered-down Italian-looking man in his early sixties, wearing a good grey suit, a white shirt with a short collar, a dark blue tie, a pair of black slip-on shoes with no hardware on the instep. He wore a flat gold watch that told the time, but not the date, or the weather, or the stock market prices.

"Pleased to meet you, Mr. Rainey," he said in a hoarse voice. He didn't look much like a mobster, but the voice put him in perspective. I don't know where they get those voices, but they have them. Subdued though it was, it was the real McCoy, and it required no stretch of

6

imagination to see him taking the Fifth in front of a subcommittee made up of publicity-seeking senators aquiver with righteous indignation.

There were bottles and glasses and an ice bucket on the glass-topped writing desk, one of those hotel desks nobody ever writes at. I asked Albergo if he wanted a drink and he said maybe a scotch and water.

"A little scotch, a lot of water," he said.

I fixed the drink and gave it to him. I'd been having Jack Daniels on the rocks. I added ice to it and sat down. Albergo leaned back in his chair, crossed his ankles, sipped his drink. Then, discarding the relaxed pose, he put down his drink and leaned forward, grinding his hands together.

"I need your help, Mr. Rainey. Your name was given to me by a man high up in the Tax and Alcohol Division. That's Federal. I guess you know that."

I did. I wasn't a bootlegger and I paid my taxes, so their knowledge of me had to be connected with the guns I'd been known to smuggle from time to time. Tax and Alcohol has a special interest in the flow of automatic weapons, which happen to be a big part of my business.

Albergo said, "My friend tells me you're a mercenary, the best in the business. He says you don't work cheap, but usually get results."

I said, "Tell me what you want, Mr. Albergo. Then we'll go on from there."

"Okay. You know who I am?"

"I know what the newspapers say."

"It doesn't bother you what I do?"

"Why should it bother me? I don't work for

you. So far we're just having a drink."

It was a New York July and the city steamed under a layer of smog. The central air-conditioning whispered soothingly. I knew Albergo had come to offer me a job, and I hoped he wouldn't be too disappointed when I told him I didn't do contract hits. Murder for money is not in my line, and neither is working for governments that would like to see the United States pulled down and rolled in the dirt. I waited for Albergo to get on with it.

"In a nutshell," he said, "my son has been an MIA—missing in action—since seventy-five, and now I get a letter from him saying he's alive and it's really him writing to let me know. I haven't seen the kid in fifteen years and you can imagine how I felt when the letter came. All these years I accepted he was dead, then—bam!—out of the blue comes this letter. His handwriting—I'd know it anywhere—no swindle, no scam to get money out of me."

I sipped a little sour mash. "What did the letter say?"

"That he was alive. Oh yeah, that he'd lost a leg the last days of the war—that stinking Kennedy-Johnson-Nixon war!—and was very sick and wanted help so he'd be able to come home. I have the letter with me. You want to see it?"

"In a minute, Mr. Albergo. Where did the letter come from?" By now I knew what the job was and I didn't want it. I'd done my time in Vietnam—my time on the cross, as some guy said—and I never wanted to see it again. It had been a dirty, useless war directed by waffling politicians, supported by those too old to fight, and waged by inept generals. I hated it then and I hate it now. Vietnam had nothing but bad memories for me: good friends who died for nothing, the stink of graft and betrayal, dead children with gas-bloated bellies floating in canals, American "aid" teams with pink faces and tentative smiles. But there was another reason, the most important reason of all, which was that the political police over there still wanted me for "war crimes." As a Green Beret attached to the Phoenix Group, the CIA-directed assassination section, I had planned and carried out the killing of South Vietnamese known to be working with the Viet Cong. Army officers. Village chiefs. Politicians. Businessmen. This was as much a part of the war as forward combat. I wasn't proud and I wasn't ashamed of what I'd done. But the political police still had my file open.

Albergo had the letter in his hand, but I didn't reach for it. "My kid says he's up in some section of the country called The Golden Triangle." Albergo moved his finger down the first page, moving his lips as he read to himself. "Yeah, here is what he says: 'All these years I have been hiding here in the Golden Triangle. They would have caught me long ago if not for the fact that the GT is such a wild, isolated part of the country. The GT is where the borders of Vietnam, Cambodia, and Thailand come together and make a sort of a triangular shape on the map. There is absolutely no law here, Communist or any other kind. The gooks have not been able to police it, and I think there must be plenty of bribery involved, as the dope smugglers, bandits, and army deserters operate openly without getting any trouble from the authorities. After I lost my leg I was bitter and ashamed and thought I never wanted to go home, but would remain here in this awful place for the rest of my life. Now I am not a kid anymore and realize how wrong I was to cut myself off from family and friends. I came to this realization several years ago, but was never able to get a letter out. Now I think there is a good chance this letter will get to you. I hope it does because I want to get out of here so bad I can't sleep thinking about it every night. We had our fights and differences in the past, but that was because I was a dumb kid that didn't know how well off he was. Please help me, Pop. I'm sick with malaria that comes back every year when it's the rainy season and I can't make it out of here on an artificial leg. Where I am in the GT is right on the Vietnam border about forty miles east of the city of Pleiku. The closest village is Cheo Reo."

Albergo folded the letter, but kept it in his hand. "After that part there's a lot of personal stuff. You can read the whole letter when you're ready. You know, I get a kick out of the kid calling me Pop after all these years. Pop, of course, he always called me when he was small, but then later when he got to be a teenager he didn't call me nothing. It was like he didn't want to acknowledge me as his father. How do you figure kids, Mr. Rainey?"

That didn't require an answer and Albergo went on, a sentimental hoodlum wanting to talk about family matters. He was prepared to be lenient with his long-lost son. "Well, in a way you can't blame him too much. I *am* in the

10

rackets. Face it, that's what I do for a living. But how do you explain to a kid that most of my business is legit? All he sees is the other thing and he's ashamed of it. I know I'll never get the Man of the Year award, but I don't think I'm such a bad man. For one thing, I don't deal in drugs. I swear it. A lot of other things, never that. I got into my business when I was a kid and am in ever since. What was an Italian kid going to do back in the Thirties? The Irish still ran the city then and kept all the good jobs for themselves and so. . ."

I must have showed some impatience because Albergo broke off his life story and laughed. "Ah, you don't want to listen to that stuff. Get on with the story, right?"

I just nodded.

"My kid, he ran away his first year of college and enlisted in the Marines." Albergo shook his head sadly, still puzzled by the ways of wayward youth. "You better believe I was plenty mad at him. What the hell, he's a changed kid by now. Back then, though, he kept me mad all the time. The money I laid out sending him to those prep schools. One after the other and he wouldn't stay in any of them, saying the kids sneered and gave him a hard time because his old man, me, was a gangster. In those days I was more in the papers than I am now. So the little creeps knew my name, who I was. I'd try to tell him stay in school, hold your head high, consider the source when they call you names. You think he'd listen?"

It was time to call a halt to all this. "Mr Albergo," I said. "Absolutely no offense, but you've come to the wrong man. I can't take the

11

job, but I can give you the names of several men who might be interested. All good men. I wouldn't suggest them if they weren't."

I half expected him to get tough about it, but he kept his voice level. "You want to tell me why you don't want the job?"

I told him the truth. It's easy to tell the truth when there is nothing to be gained by not telling it. Skipping the bad-memories stuff, I told him about the Phoenix Group, the sanctioned murders committed as a means of furthering American Policy in that miserable, devastated country.

"I'm on a list of war criminals," I said. "I know that because I read it in a book by an Australian Communist. There are hundreds of names, he said. I just happened to be a typical example of what the Green Beret squads did over there. That was why he mentioned me in particular."

Albergo said, "It's eight years since the war ended, Mr. Rainey."

"Makes no difference. My file is active and will remain active for years. Communists don't forget. Not only that, they have my picture. Our people didn't get to burn all the files before they pulled out. So the political police know what I look like. A man doesn't change all that much in ten years. That's the last time my ID was updated."

"There must be more important people than you they're looking for."

"I'm not saying I'm important. I'm saying they have me on a list of war criminals. I go over there, there's a good chance I'll be caught. It's a closed country these days. Very few foreigners are allowed in, especially white foreigners and above all Americans. Anyway, our own government has declared it off limits. It's stamped right in your passport."

Albergo's face twitched in a faint smile. "You wouldn't let that stop you if you wanted to go?"

"If I wanted to go. I don't want to go. You know what would happen if they caught me? They wouldn't just shoot me in the basement of some police station. First would come the torture. After so many years they wouldn't be in that much of a hurry. They'd drag it out. You don't die of their kind of torture. For important prisoners they always have a doctor present. Torture has come a long way since the Chinese used it in Korea, so after the new, improved torture comes the trial, probably in front of TV cameras. You think you won't crack when they first catch you, but by the time the trial comes around, you're nothing but a babbling wreck. Better men that I am have signed phony confessions."

"I think you'd stand up, Mr. Rainey."

"How can you tell? I can't tell. The point is, I don't want to go through it. Look. I'm a mercenary and I fight in wars for the most money I can get. Usually the worst that can happen to me is getting killed. You live with that, you accept it. This other thing is altogether different. Sorry, I'd rather not do it."

Albergo wet his lips with the scotch and water. "You mentioned money just now. The most money you can get, is what you said."

"I wasn't priming the pump, if that's what you think."

"What?"

"A country expression," I said. "What I mean,

13

I wasn't setting you up for a big bite. I don't want to go over there for any kind of money."

Albergo blotted his lips with a snowy white handkerchief. "Would fifty thousand and expenses change your mind?"

"It's not the money," I said.

"Come on, Mr. Rainey, it's always the money."

I liked the little mobster in spite of what he was. Who could doubt that in his time he had killed men, or had them killed, after he became a top Mafia executive? But that didn't bother me very much. I've never kept count of the men who died in front of my gun, but the total had to be greater than Joseph Albergo's. Most mobsters are weasels; a few are men of honor—within reason, that is. In my business you learn to take men as they are, never making snap judgements unless the guy is all too obviously a son of a bitch.

"I'm not hurting for money," I told the little mobster. "I just got back from a job in Asia and still have most of what I was paid. I could go a year without working if I wanted to."

"But you won't?"

"Probably not."

Albergo took another little drink. I wondered if his tiny drinks had anything to do with his size. He still clutched his son's letter in his left hand. A link with the unhappy past, one he didn't want to break.

"You mind telling me what you got for the Asia job?"

"Twenty thousand. Not a lot, but I've got a few bucks in the bank."

Albergo said, "A hundred thousand is five times more than that."

14

"You said fifty a minute ago."

"Now I'm saying a hundred," Albergo said. "I don't want to argue price like some Arab on Atlantic Avenue. You get expenses with the hundred thousand. That's a hundred thousand clear. In cash. No taxes unless you want to pay them. Nobody has to know a single dollar has changed hands."

I shook my head. "I don't want to do it and I'm not trying to hold you up for more money. The mercs I mentioned, they're all good men and they don't have hanging over them what's hanging over me. There's one guy I know for sure won't turn you down. For fifty thousand he'd break into the Kremlin."

Albergo waved his hand. "The guy sounds too reckless, maybed nuts. I don't want a reckless guy. What I want is a guy that does it cool and does it right. I'm told that's you. As for holding me up, I don't mind that. You're in a dangerous business and have to look out for yourself. Cards on the table, Mr. Rainey. Tell me what you want and I'll tell you what I think."

The little man was as hard to put off as a drunken sailor trying to get into a whorehouse after closing time. I didn't want to tell him to get lost, because mobsters can get tetchy, and when they get really tetchy, usually they send some of the boys around to teach the offending party manners. The last thing I wanted was to go back to Texas on crutches.

"I told you it's not the money," I said again. "If I wanted to go, I'd name a price and that would be it. No bargaining, no cute moves. If that guy in Tax and Alcohol knows anything about me, then he must have told you that."

"He did," Albergo said. " A hundred and fifty? You

15

see I go up by fifties."

"Not interested."

"Two hundred," Albergo said. "There I stop because it's too much at that figure. This time don't answer so fast. Think about it."

"I'm thinking about something else. Let me ask you a question. You're connected, must have contacts everywhere. Then why can't you use people in your own organization to handle this? I'm not saying use Americans, but what about organization people in the Far East? There shouldn't be any problem finding qualified people in Hong Kong, Manila, Singapore. I've worked with Chinese and Filipino mercs and they're as good as any American."

"No good," Albergo said. "I don't mean the mercs, I mean the suggestion. You're the man I want to bring out my son."

"But why? I told you there are men just as reliable."

"That's not the reason."

"Then why?"

"Because I really don't think the money comes first with you."

"That's what you think," I said. "No money, no job. I always collect."

"Sure you do," Albergo said. "But I think the life is what appeals to you, not the money. It's great to make big money. Besides, it gives you an excuse to do what you do. Where else could I make this kind of money? you ask yourself. In the mercenary business, you answer. But in the end, it's the life, not the money, that draws you to danger. Correct me if I'm wrong, Mr. Rainey."

"I think it's a little of both," I said. "What difference does it make?"

"It could make a difference when you think about it. If you turn me down and I leave, there won't be another offer, and maybe you'll wonder if you did the right thing. My Tax and Alcohol friend says you're the gutsiest, most daring merc anywhere. He says you do things other people think are impossible. This guy wouldn't lie to me." Albergo paused. "He knows better than that when it's a thing with my son."

"What are you getting at, Mr. Albergo?"

"What I'm getting at is I think later you'll be sorry if you turn down this job. What was the real reason? you'll ask yourself. Was it because it was a really difficult job, or was I plain scared? You're an honest man, so you'll give yourself the right answer. Then you'll think, hey, if I'm scared of the Vietnam job, how about the job after that, the job I do take? It's not so good for a man in your line of work to be scared."

"You're saying it, not me."

"No offense, Mr. Rainey, but you know I'm right. Get scared a little, you end up by getting scared a lot. Let me tell you a story, not a long one. Back in Thirty-five, I came through a gang war, a real bloody thing with tough Jews trying to move into New York from Brooklyn. Thing went on for months, dead guys all over the place. I was in the thick of it all that time and never once did I lose my nerve. I was wounded twice and came close to dying. But that didn't stop me. Soon as I was able to lift a sawed-off shotgun I was back out there on the street, blasting away. Like I say, I came through the war, then there was a big sitdown and a truce was declared. Nothing was done in good faith

17

so the truce didn't last. The war started up again and I was one of the top troops, only this time, you know, only a month later, I was nervous about getting killed and I didn't want to fight anymore. I'd lost my nerve. I was scared."

"What happened?"

"Well, to get to the point, I got a call from Dominic Mora, one of my bosses—he's dead now—and the word from him is the big Jew that started the war always eats his dinner in a delicatessen in Crown Heights and they want me to be part of the hit team. I started shaking when I heard that. Crown Heights was Jew territory in those days and we'd be like Custer taking on the five thousand Sioux. Well, you know, I could have got out of it, having been wounded twice already and not fully recovered, which was more or less the truth. God Almighty! I didn't want to go to Crown Heights for any reason, never mind going there to make a hit."

"But you went."

"Yeah, I went all right, but at first I thought they'd have to carry me there. The hit was scheduled for eight o'clock the next evening, so I had a whole day to think about it, how scared I was. A couple of times I picked up the phone and started to dial Dominic and tell him I was all crippled up with muscle spasms from the gunshot wounds. Dominic wouldn't have said a thing, after what I'd been through. But I just couldn't cop out, couldn't hide from the danger, because I knew I'd never again be any good if I did. The guys I went over there with got killed but I kept on shooting till I wasted the Jew and his four bodyguards. It had to be done, so I did it. A hard way to get over being scared.

It was worth it."

I smiled at the diminutive mobster. The story might be nothing but bullshit. Just the same, he had scored a few points. Two hundred thousand was a huge sum of money, even for me, and I hated to pass it up.

Albergo had needled me where it hurt and I'd have to think things over. Fear is what all mercs are afraid of, and with them the fear of fear is stronger that it is with regular soldiers, who have no choice but to go into battle when they're ordered to. It's different with mercs, because they don't have to be there at all. They hire out for money. Nobody forces them to sign contracts; they could just as well go home and get jobs as security guards.

"Will you at least think about it?" Albergo said. "Got you a little shook up, haven't I?"

"I'll think about it," I said. "You have a number where you can be reached?"

Albergo wrote the number on the back of one of the message slips from the front desk. "That's where I live," he said. "I'll be home all evening. Call anytime up to midnight. That's when I take my baby Phenobarb. A hell of a thing when you can't sleep, only I don't mind so much not being able to sleep these days because I'm thinking about my kid coming home. Fifteen years, can you imagine that? Not a word, not a letter in all that time. When he ran off from college, the ground might as well have opened and swallowed him. Call one way or another, Mr. Rainey. Good news or bad, I'd like to have a definite answer."

"I'll call for sure," I said.

Albergo left and I made myself a big drink. I sat close to the window and looked out over Manhattan. I could have seen a good part of New Jersey, if

I'd been interested.

I smiled, recalling Albergo's story. There had been no need to lay in on so thick. But he was right: right now I was asking myself questions.

Was I being sensible about the Vietnam job? Or was I scared. To go to Vietnam meant putting myself in the way of a horrible death. I would die by inches, mutilated, my brain destroyed, my nervous system shattered beyond repair. There would be days and nights, weeks and perhaps months of agony, and in all that time I would beg for death, and it wouldn't come quick because they weren't ready.

Nothing seemed more sensible than to avoid all that by refusing the job. After a month or so in Texas, I'd probably start looking for something new to work on. Hell, I'd go back and do what I'd been doing all along. So what was this "scared" shit?

After I had another drink, I knew I was kidding myself, or trying to. The whisky must have loosened me up, made me see the truth. Whiskey can do that in the early stages of a night's drinking. You're scared to go over there, sonny, I told myself. Being sensible has nothing to do with it. Then I tried to explain to myself that there was such a thing as being scared of one situation but not of another. That helped for a while, then the truth raised its ugly head and bawled me out for being a liar, a hypocrite, and a coward.

I had left Vietnam ten years before and I still hated the memory of the place. Nothing good about it came to mind, though I tried hard to think of some redeeming feature. Good friends had died there, some bravely, some not. It hardly mattered how they died; they had no business there in the first place.

Joe Albergo was right: I had to go back or I'd

always wonder about myself. The courage bit gives me a pain in the ass, but even so, some of the cliches have a grain of truth in them. I guess I was getting a little drunk.

I dialed Albergo's number and he answered on the first ring. "Yes, Mr. Rainey?" he said.

"I've decided to take the job at two hundred thousand."

"That's good to hear," Albergo said. "I'll see you tomorrow."

TWO

NEXT DAY , at noon, Joseph Albergo came to my hotel with fifty thousand in cash. Along with the money he brought the letter and a photograph of his son made shortly before he went into the Marines.

"I wonder what he looks like now," Albergo said. "He used to be a real good-looking kid, which proves he didn't take after his father, right? And he's tall, about as tall as you are. How tall are you?"

"Six feet even."

Albergo, happier now, stepped back to look at me. "Yeah, I'd say my kid's as tall as you. Poor kid, I mean losing the leg. Well, it could be worse, thank God. A lot of guys came back paraplegics from that rotten war. I used to get into arguments with an Irish guy that lived next door then. American Legion, I think he was, or maybe Veterans of Foreign Wars. We have to stop Communism some time, some place, he used to say. Or else we'll be fighting them on the West Coast."

"Guys like that always say that." I wanted to get

rid of him.

There was a lot to be done and I wanted to get to it. Mr. Albergo, I hope you don't mind. I have to see about a couple of things. You want me to call you before I leave?"

Albergo looked a little sad as if he wanted to come along. "No," he said. "You don't have to do that." We shook hands, then he held onto my hand so long, it got embarrassing. "You do this for me, Mr. Rainey, and I'll never forget you as long as I live. Bring my kid back safe and sound and there's no favor you can't ask Joe Albergo."

"I'll do my best," I said.

Soon after he left, I went over to the Rand McNally store on East 45th Street and bought all the detailed maps of Indochina they had in stock. Then, on the way back to the hotel, I deposited forty-five of the fifty thousand in a safe deposit box I've had for years.

Back at the hotel, I spread the maps out on the bed and studied them. The Golden Triangle! What lousy memories the name brought back. One week the VC had it; the week after we took it back. And so it went all through the war. The odd thing is, that even with a bloody war going on, in spite of all the bombing and shelling, the lice that infested the Triangle refused to be driven out. Some old major who'd been a history instructor at the War College told me the Triangle had been like that for centuries.

Albergo's son was telling it like it was when he described the Triangle as absolutely lawless. But I was surprised to hear that the Communists hadn't been able to do anything about it. Asian Communists are the most puritanical of all, forever seeking out sin.

After looking at the maps, I knew I'd have to go in through Saigon, now called Ho Chi Minh City. As a U.S. citizen I couldn't enter Vietnam under any name. Australians and New Zealanders also were barred because they had sent troops to the war. Canada had not, so it was possible for someone to enter the country on a Canadian passport. I was about to become a Canuck.

Getting a fake passport was no big deal. I knew a printer in Brooklyn who could supply *anything*: passports, college diplomas, driver's licenses. You name it, he could print it. I had used him before many times and knew his work held up under close scrutiny.

But I decided to go the straight route and get a real Canadian passport. It's not hard to work. You go to any cemetery in Canada and look around for a headstone with a baby's name on it. When you find it, you go to the registrar of births and deaths and apply for a birth certificate, using the baby's name. Once you get the birth certificate, you're all set to apply for a passport. Crooks and spies do it all the time.

I had to have a cover, a reason for wanting to enter Vietnam. Hardly the do-gooder type, I thought I might pass as a newspaperman. Why not? The journalists I'd seen in Vietnam during the war had done little more than drink. They wrote their best on-the-scene stories in the bars on Vanel Street. But the cover would have to be good; the political police would check.

I had to establish myself as a Canadian journalist, preferably left-leaning, to make it look good. Getting a passport was the easiest part of it. It was when I applied for a visa that the spotlight would be turned on me. They'd check and recheck before they gave me permission to enter Vietnam, and even if I did check out, they might say no. If that happened, I'd have to start all over again.

The Vietnamese have no embassy in Canada; there isn't even a consulate. Everything has to go through the Russians. Vietnam used to be a "client state" of China. Now it's a "client state" of Russia. Vietnam and China fell out a few years ago, mainly because of the persecution of Chinese minorities who looked to the homeland for guidance, and the Russians were only too glad to step in and look after the foreign affairs of their little yellow brothers. The KGB would run the first check, then the Viet political police would go to work on me.

Albergo Senior wanted me to get on my pogo stick, but I wasn't ready to be rushed. His son had been missing in action for fifteen years; a few more weeks weren't going to make much difference.

Real life isn't a bit like the movies, not even the ones with dirty talk and grainy photography. If this were the movies I'd hire a daredevil pilot and parachute into the Triangle, find Joe Albergo Junior and bundle him across the border—to where? We'd fly in low to fool the radar, and never mind the soldiers and farmers and villagers that were sure to spot us. We'd last about ten minutes if we did that. The Vietnamese have an air force now, mostly overage MIG's they keep in top condition, and they have all the anti-aircraft guns and rocket systems they need, most of them abandoned by the Americans when we pulled out in seventy-five.

I hadn't shaved that morning; in a week I would have a fine set of whiskers. Contact lenses would change the color of my eyes. I went over to an optician's in the theater district and came out with brown eyes (my own are pale blue) and a pair of horn-rims with clear glass in them.

Years before in Nam I'd caught a shell splinter in the leg. An ugly scar remained but I was able to walk without limping. It was all right to carry a cane, one more detail that might help to convince them that I was nothing more than what I'd seem to be: a forty year-old, slightly decrepit Canadian journalist who worked for a little known magazine or newspaper with a leftist bias.

I bought a cane at a luggage and umbrella store on Broadway and walked around for a while to get the feel of it. What I was putting together wasn't really a disguise but an altering of my appearance. But it has to go deeper than that if you hope to be successful. When you buy a cane to change how you look, you don't just go tap-tap and forget about the rest of it. A man who carries a cane for a long time uses it as a sort of extension of his arm. He uses it to move things, to hail taxis, to point when strangers ask him directions. It has to become part of him, not just a prop like a false beard or elevator heels.

I'm tall; the cane helped me to stoop a little. Some of my East Texas accent remains, but that was no problem. Most Americans and Canadians sound the same, especially to foreigners. But the name I picked from some dead infant's grave had to fit my appearance.

The Canadian Passport Department might not show any interest, but the Vietnamese might get suspicious if I showed up in Saigon as Aristotle Aristophanes or Mohammed Ben Barka. Ethnic names were out because I might run into some foreign Communist, Polish or Hungarian or Latvian, with too many questions about where my folks came from. My best bet was to go East as Patrick Murphy, Angus McGregor, Dickie Jones, or Reginald Briggs. There had to be dead babies in Canada with names like that.

I stayed in New York until my beard grew out. It came out streaked with grey, making me look older than I was, so I decided to up my age to forty-five when I applied for the passport. By then I'd moved to another hotel, so old man Albergo couldn't check up on me and maybe decide I was dragging my feet. I'd warned him not to have me tailed and he said he wouldn't think of doing such a thing. We were friends and he trusted me and how I did the job was entirely up to me. Even so, I did some fast footwork.

During that week of waiting I did without booze or women. I went to Social Sciences section of the main public library to read up on what Vietnam is like today. Most of the books and articles I read were written by "neutrals": Swedes, Italians, Indians, Canadians. Americans, Australians, and New Zealanders are persona non grata.

There was no need to read about the war: I'd been there and knew all I needed to know. But it gave me a strange feeling to read about familiar places, the scenes of ambushes and battles, that were now said to be centers of light industry. Or that new cities had sprung up to take the place of war-shattered villages, that there was a vast new rubber plantation in what had been a vast malarial swamp.

The only recent information on the Golden Triangle I found in a Canadian weekly magazine. According to the article, the writer not only had managed to penetrate the Triangle but had interviewed several of its leading bad men. One in particular was a German ex-GI who boasted that it would take a full-scale offensive by the Vietnamese army to clear the Triangle of its criminals, deserters, bandits, and heroin smugglers.

I wasn't sure I believed everything in the article, but the writer did hit a few notes that sounded true. He wrote: "I believe the Golden Triangle exists only because the Vietnamese Government allows it to exist. Rugged though the terrain is, it could be brought under control by a concerted effort on the part of the military. If the Vietnamese Communists could force the Americans to retire, it stands to reason that they could subdue a few thousand renegades. However, it seems as if Government leaders have decided that such a drive simply isn't worth it. In time, after the country has been rebuilt, they will surely change their minds and move against this lawless enclave. For the moment, they have adopted a policy of hands off. For them, and especially for their military and political intelligence services, the Golden Triangle must have its uses. It sits squarely on the borders of three countries—Vietnam, Laos and Cambodia—and no doubt serves as an invaluable source of information. Last but not least, the reluctance of the Vietnamese Government to clean out the Golden Triangle must be due in part to corruption in high places."

I read about Vietnam until I was sick of it. Then a week after I took Joseph Albergo's money I flew to Toronto, checked into a hotel just long enough to buy clothes and shoes with Canadian labels, and visited the public library, where I searched through the newspaper obituaries for 1938. After an hour of cranking the handle of the microflim viewer I found a kid named William Malcolm Stewart who had died on February 12th of that year. "He will live forever in our hearts," the obit promised. His grieving parents were listed as Knox J. and Mildred.

My next move was to check on what kind of people they were. The name Knox J. Stewart meant nothing to me; he could be the mayor of Toronto or a notorious criminal by now; the passport department people might call the cops if I walked in claiming to be his son.

There was only one Knox J. Stewart in the phone book, which gave his address as 237 Abercrombie Street. I didn't know the city; it could be Park Avenue or the Lower East Side. I dialed and got a woman with a Scottish accent. I asked for Mr. Knox and he came to the phone. He had a Scottish accent too, rough and hoarse and irritable.

"What is it ye wanted?" he growled. A TV set was squawking in the background.

"I hope I'm not disturbing you, Mr. Stewart," I started off. "But the Conservative Party is conducting a telephone poll and..."

Knox J. Stewart jumped all over me. "Ah, if

ye had a lick of sense, mon, ye'd go to yer files and see I never voted for the Conservatives in me life. I been a working man for close on fifty years an' want no truck with you nor yer bloody Conservatives. Good day to ye, sir." He hung up in my ear. So far, so good.

I got a birth certificate by filling out a form and paying a fee of six dollars. Nobody in the Registry of Births and Deaths gave me a second look. I rented a furnished apartment for a month and gave that as my home address when I applied for a passport. The man I spoke to took the filled-out form and the two passport photos and said it would take a week to ten days. He said they could mail the passport or I could pick it up in person. I said I'd call for it.

"A week to ten days," he repeated.

I figured it would be a month before I got out of Toronto. It might be longer than that, but I wasn't going to hang around until my beard turned white. There was plenty to do; a passport wasn't enough. I needed a driver's license and the other odds and ends you usually find in a man's wallet. Laundry tickets, old business cards from salesmen, that sort of thing.

All this sounds like dull, plodding work, and it was. But everything I did to shape my new identity might help save my life. If I'd been a part of some intelligence agency, everything would have been handled by specialists in deception. No matter, I did the best I could.

Little by little, I put it together.

There was a coffee shop near my apartment where salesmen pinned their business cards to a corkboard. I took two. A newsprint salesman and a guy who traveled for an office equipment company. I wrote the title of a new history of Vietnam on the back of the paper salesman's card. The personality I was trying for was that of a slightly disorganized journalist, competent when it came to his work but not too good at taking care of the details of everyday life. How well this would work remained to be seen.

I plodded on. Cheap shirts were bought and checked into a Chinese laundry; at the motor vehicles office I got a learner's permit and asked if they could push up my road test, because I had urgent business overseas. In the States I might have tried to see how much magic a fifty-dollar bill can work, but this was Canada, where bribery is not a way of life, and a kind offer of half a yard might land me in jail. The woman behind the counter had an English-Canadian accent, one of those unreconstructed Empire loyalists who was sure to have a colored photograph of the Queen in the living room, and she asked me where I was going. I told her I was a freelance writer going to Northern Ireland to write a long piece, perhaps a book, on the war.

"Mr. Stewart," she said, glancing at my application form. "Don't you think the Irish are perfectly dreadful? All that senseless killing! Why can't they be content to be British? I should think they'd consider it an honor."

I wanted that road test as fast as I could get it. "Confidentially," I said lowering my voice and leaning forward on my stick, "I can't stand them myself. They'll never be fit to govern themselves no matter who's in power. Britain has been too lenient with them if you ask me. But Mrs. Thatcher knows how to deal with them."

I added Mrs. Thatcher because this brittle

broad did look like the Iron Lady, nemesis of the Argentines. She touched her hand to her rinsed auburn hair and smiled at me.

"Indeed she does," she said.

She would have gone on with this moronic conversation if there hadn't been a line of people behind me. "Be careful over there, Mr. Stewart," she warned before I went to another room to take the written part of the test. "Oh, Mr. Stewart, call me about your road test. Ask for Mrs. McCausland. I'm sure we'll be able to accommodate you."

I still hadn't figured out how I was going to establish myself as a Toronto journalist. Meanwhile, I did lesser chores. Toronto was a city I didn't know very well, though I'd been there a number of times in the past. So I bought a city map and a guide book and strolled around. I did that for several days until I had the layout of the city in my head. More or less. It takes a lifetime to really know a big city. I had only a month. A month was what I gave myself, knowing that it might not be enough. But there was no way to hurry the Russians or the Vietnamese. They're as unpredictable as a paranoid speed freak and they never give reasons for saying yes or saying no. My visa application might go into the bureaucratic mill, never to be heard of again. There it might languish in some dusty corner until somebody finally got around to making a decision. In their way, the Russians are as Asian as the Vietnamese; there is the same disregard for time, the same implacable patience, the same conviction that all they have to do is wait and events will turn in their favor.

I read the newspaper, I watched television. There was a very old tavern on Yonge Street where newspapermen came to drink their lunch and all other meals. There I soaked up shop talk: papers threatened by union trouble, libel suits, a new city editor brought in from the West, the good-looking feminist reporter who wouldn't put out and was probably a frigging lesbian, the latest antics of some legendary drunk.

Shop talk didn't take up all their time. Mostly what they talked about was money, women, ice hockey, betting, booze. They compared hangovers, suggested cures. No one took any notice of me. I was of no importance and they knew it. Celebrity faces are everything to a reporter; my face rang no bell.

But I did get talking to a few of them, and that was usually after they'd been drinking awhile. Most newsmen are naturally, or professionally, gregarious and they seldom hesitate before they ask personal questions. So many doors have been slammed in their faces that anything less than a kick in the balls is not enough to turn them off.

A few guys nodded to me after I'd been going there for a few days, usually in mid-afternoon after the lunch crowd had gone. One afternoon, halfway through my week of waiting for the passport, I got talking to a skinny, poorly dressed guy on the sour side of sixty, one of those steady drinkers that are never quite sober. He was Ike Lasker, I was Bill Stewart. Somehow I got the idea that he didn't work for any of the regular newspapers. Something was missing; I decided it was aggressiveness, without which most newsmen can't function.

I was drinking Molson's ale, he was nursing a scotch and water, trying to make it last. The bartender closest to us didn't seem to approve of him. Now and then one of the reporters would give him a condescending hello that was often accompanied by a wink for the amusement of the other boozers.

"Haven't see you here before," he said. "No, that isn't right. I saw you yesterday. New in town?"

"From out West. British Columbia," I said.

"Let me guess what you do. You don't look like a newspapermen. You're a teacher, right?"

"Used to teach high school," I said, not trying to reach too high in the academic world. "Stuck it for twenty years, then took early retirement."

I didn't think this conversation was going anywhere. But what the hell! Like a Method actor I was trying to get inside the skin of this fictitious person, William Malcolm Stewart.

Ike Lasker took a short swallow of his long, weak drink. His eyes were tired. "What would you peg me as?" he wanted to know. "Seeing me as I am, what would you take me for?"

It didn't make much a difference what I said. "Maybe a rewrite man. No, you review movies."

Ike Lasker gave out with a wheezing laugh that made me think of emphysema. "Wrong on both accounts. I'm a publisher. What do you think of that?"

Nothing about him told me he was a rich eccentric. Maybe he published one of those flimsy throw-away news sheets you see in supermarkets.

"What do you publish?" I asked. "Maybe I should know, but I haven't been in town very long."

Ike Lasker grimaced. "No reason why you should have heard of me in British Columbia. But once upon a time I did carve a little niche for myself in Toronto. My little newspaper, *Progressive World*, stood up to the Canadian brand of McCarthyism when all the other papers kept

34

papers kept their heads buried in the sand, when they weren't openly supporting the right-wing sons of bitches."

"Oh yes," I said, "I remember hearing about it."

"Then you must have been a smart kid, an interested kid. That was thirty years ago. Our native McCarthyites came along at exactly the right time, with the country still terrified of Communists after the big spy scare of the late Forties. Funny, you're right about the rewrite part. That's what I did before they bounced me off the paper as a security risk! What kind of nonsense is that? A rewrite man a security risk! But I tell you I was glad to go. I'm no Communist, but try to explain that at the time. I don't know what your politics are, but I happen to be a socialist, or I used to be."

"You mean you've given up on it?"

"Yeah, I suppose you could say that. These days I just go through the motions. I'm getting old and don't care much anymore. Nobody else cares, why should I? But there was a time when I thought my little paper was going to turn into a journal of influence."

"How did it get started?" An idea was forming in my mind. "It must take money to start any kind of paper."

"Not that much money. It was a very small paper, even smaller now. My mother died and I sold the house. I had some money saved and, then there was the money I got back from the pension fund. Friends chipped in. It got started. It did poorly in the Fifties, though it did get attention. The Sixties were much better because the paper took a strong anti-Vietnam War position and we gave the Americans hell at every opportunity. You probably get along with the

Americans out West, but here they're not too popular."

"We're not crazy about them either."

Ike Lasker sighed, a man living in the past. "Probably not."

His glass was nearly empty. "Let me buy you a drink," I said. "I have to stay with beer because my doctor won't let me drink the hard stuff."

"All right," Ike Lasker said. "Nothing serious, I hope."

The bartender gave us the drinks.

"Then, you know," Ike Lasker said, "people got sick of the war. It went on too long and people got tired of even hearing about it. The old war, World War II, was so different. They call it the last just war, and I guess it was. Good guys, bad guys. The choice was easy to make. The Nazis had to be destroyed, so we all pitched in. Even I was in the service, though I never got any closer to the war than Novia Scotia."

"But you still publish," I said.

"I still publish, for what it's worth. I go through the motions. It's something to keep me busy. I guess you're wondering how I can keep the paper going. The answer is the printer, an old time socialist, prints it for next to nothing. Sometimes for nothing at all. It depends how much is in the bank account. I write every word that goes into it: news items, editorials, articles."

"Under a lot of different names?"

"What else? I have to preserve the fiction that it's a real newspaper and not just a crank sheet turned out byone man. But I'm really fooling nobidy, anyway not this crowd in here. They think I'm a nut. Do you think I'm a nut?"

I shook my head. "No, I don't think you're a

nut." I was thinking of all the pseudonyms Lasker used in his newspaper.

"One thing you have to say for *Progressive World*," Ike Lasker said, mildly boastful, "it hasn't missed an edition for close to thirty years. Certainly nothing special for any other paper, for my paper it is. You know how many small papers are born and die in thirty years? I can think of a dozen. But we always hung in there and the paper got out one way or another."

I insisted on buying him another drink.

After he drank some of it I said, " You got any kind of staff now?"

He smiled as if he remembered the days when he had a real staff. "Depends on what you mean by a staff. A couple of old Socialist ladies my age help out when they can. Typing, proofreading, trying to get ads. There used to be a hippie kid gave me a hand, but he kept trying to sneak pro-drug editorials past me and I had to get rid of him. The staff is me. I write everything under different names. I try to vary the style. It's hard. Tell you the truth, Bill, I'd like to sell the damned thing and go fishing."

"I suppose you could do that," I said.

THREE

"IF YOU really wanted to do it, you could probably
find a buyer," I said. "But it sounds like you've
got your whole life wrapped up in this paper.
After all these years, how can you just let it go?"

Ike Lasker wasn't so shy about drinking his second free drink. "Easy," he said, fiddling with the
swizzle stick. "I'm tired of socialism. Who cares?
We'll all be blown to kingdom comes in a few
years. It won't even be a war. A monumental
goof-up will bring about the end of the world.
If it can go wrong, it will. Murphy's Law. The
same thing applies to nuclear weapons."

"Let's hope not," I said.

"Yeah," Ike Lasker said, "let's hope not. You
know, I'm not kidding about selling the paper,
not that it would bring that much. But it does
have a name that, well, some people will
recognize, and it has been around for thirty
years. It even had some powerful enemies when
it was at its best, in the Sixties. Questions were
asked about it in Parliament. *Pravda* quoted it
occasionally, not that I was so happy about that.
The *Progressive World* has some name

recognition."

We moved to a table when some people left. The bar was dark and air-conditioned, much quieter than it would have been at lunchtime. There was no jukebox, so it wasn't necessary to shout.

I said, "What would you consider to be a fair selling price?"

Ike Lasker was surprised. "You interested? I thought we were just talking. At least I was. What would you do with that kind of paper?"

"I'm not sure. Maybe give it a new slant. I'm interested in the New Social-Democrat party in the UK. Socialism with a difference. Why not? Everything else has been tried."

Ike Lasker looked me over. "You have that kind of money?"

"What kind of money, Ike? You haven't said how much you want for the paper."

"I hadn't really thought it out. I have to be honest with you. There's no plant. That belongs to the printer. The office these days is one floor in a small loft building. Everything in the office is the property of the paper: desks, typewriters, a Thermafax copying machine. The usual. You'll be buying a name and nothing else."

"I understand," I said. "How much?"

"I don't know. Is five thousand to much?"

"No, I can swing that."

"What did you have in mind? A bank loan?"

"No, I'll give you a certified check for the full amount. Naturally I'd like to look over your operation before we firm up the sale. The banks are closed now. We can get our business finished tomorrow if everything checks out today."

Ike Lasker finished his drink. "There's not a

lot to check out."

"Then let's go check it."

"You want to have your accountant go over the books?"

"I have no accountant, and no lawyer. Let's keep this simple, one man to another. You get a check for five thousand and I don't take possession until it's cashed or cleared by the bank. We'll write out a simple agreement and we'll both sign it and have it notarized. That okay with you?"

Things were moving too fast for Ike Lasker. The old socialist newspaper was his only asset. It wasn't worth five thousand to anyone but me. I knew I could have knocked him down to twenty-five hundred, but why fool around when I was getting so much from Albergo?

"Couldn't be better," Ike Lasker said. "What do you have, Bill? A rich uncle, a rich wife? I know what they pay high school teachers."

"A rich girlfriend is what I have, Ike."

Ike Lasker swigged the last of his drink. "What about another one to celebrate?"

"When we close the deal," I said.

The offices of the *Progressive World* were only a short distance away, on a back street that was mostly warehouses. Ike Lasker led me around the back of a trailer truck parked on the broken sidewalk, then up a flight of concrete steps to the second floor of a building that smelled of dry rot and mouse droppings. There was a door with *Progressive World* lettered on it; IKE LASKER/EDITOR & PUBLISHER was the second line; Est. 1954 was lettered at the bottom.

Sounds of typing came through the frosted glass door, and when we went in, two stout ladies were pounding away on old manual Royals in an outer office. Old stacks of the *Progressive World* were piled high on shelves, on the floor, on several wooden tables. An ancient air-conditioner made as much noise as an automobile engine with a broken fan belt. A battered coffee pot belched on top of a two-burner hotplate. There was a burly refrigerator, an outdated copying machine, three chairs, a coat rack.

Ike Lasker introduced me as Bill Stewart from British Columbia. The stout socialist ladies nodded, curious but polite. Both were in their sixties, no doubt veterans of many demonstrations in the murky past. I think they adored nervous, booze-rattled, nicotine-stained Ike Lasker.

We went into his private office and he closed the door. "What you see is what's here." Ike Lasker laughed. "That sounds silly, doesn't it? What I mean is, there's no more than meets the eye. I have no important debts because no one will lend me money. Any debts I do owe are personal and not connected with the paper. If you're concerned that the printer will try to collect monies due from the past, forget it. However, you will have to make your own arrangements with the printer. Format, press run, all that will have to be discussed with him. There's always the chance that he may not want to keep the account. There are other printers..."

I had to shut him up. "That's my problem," I said. "I don't see there's much more to discuss. You want to dictate a paper of agreement to one of the ladies out there? They can witness it and that'll do as good as a notary. Then in the

41

morning we'll meet at the bank and finalize the deal. That suit you?"

"Down to the ground." Ike Lasker looked happy, then a wistful look came to his eyes. "There's no chance you'd want to keep me on as an editor? At a regular salary, I mean. You wouldn't have to pay me much. I could show you the ropes."

"Sorry, Ike," I said, clapping him on the arm. "I'm like you. I intend to run a one-man show."

The stout ladies cried when Ike Lasker broke the bad news to them. Then they got mad at him after they thought about it. Ike was showing the white flag after all those years in the fray. He cowered a little under their disapproving stares.

"It's time for a younger man to take up the banner," Ike Lasker said piously. "We have fought the good fight. That at least we can be proud of."

The ladies asked me if I intended to carry on the traditions and policies of the *Progressive World*. No, I said, something different was on the drawing board.

The ladies stalked out, leaving me with Ike Lasker. "I'll give you the keys when you give me the check," he said.

We shook hands and I went back to my apartment. A chance meeting in a bar had solved the problem of how to pass myself off as a Canadian journalist. Now I had an employment record: I'd been writing for the *Progressive World* for many years. Tomorrow, after I got the keys, I would sit down and read back issues of the paper. Ike Lasker had written everything in the paper, using a dozen names, maybe more than that. I had my choice of pseudonyms. I could be one writer or many. It might work with a little extra planning.

Next morning I met Ike Lasker at the bank. He'd been having a few, But he was sober enough. I got a cashier's chek for five thousand and gave it to him. This was the most money he'd seen for a lot of years. He deposited the check and bought a book of traveler's checks. Then we went to a bar to have a farewell drink. He let me pay.

"I really am going fishing," he told me. "Isn't it an odd thing? With all the wide open spaces we have in Canada I haven't been out of the city in thirty years. The suburbs, sure, but never out where the buffalo roam."

"You sure the fresh air won't kill you?" I wasn't just making light conversation; this guy's plans were of some concern to me, and it wouldn't be so great if he started coming around the office when he got loaded. He was a talkative man. He might talk to the wrong people.

"I may not do that much fishing," he went on. "More what I envisage is renting a cabin by a lake where I can drink unbothered by bill collecters and elderly socialist ladies who want to take care of me. There is a certain widow of considerable means, but never mind that. I may try to write a book about the failure of orthodox socialism. Then again I may not. Who in hell would want to read it? In the meantime, I shall drink. Fortunately, I am able to control it."

"How long do you think you'll be gone?"

"Probably till the fall. It will be a tonic for me to get away from this Scotch Presbyterian city for a while. Toronto like to think it's cosmopolitain, but its heart's still in the Highlands. When the snows come I'll have to give some serious thought to my friend the widow. May I drop in on you when I return? A series of articles, perhaps? This Social Democrat busniess, I haven't kept up with it, but I'm a quick study."

"Sure," I said. "Drop me a line so I'll know how you're getting on. You have any particular place in mind?"

"A little place called Argyle Station, a few miles from North Bay, is where I'm going." Ike Lasker's faded eyes got a dreamy look in them, and I wasn't sure how long his so-called controlled drinking was going to last now that he had money. Already he was letting himself go; his manner had grown expansive, his speech stilted.

"In the Thirties there was a little socialist cooperative there, but it failed." Ike Lasker waved his hand, dismissing the communal experiment. "Call it a sentimental journey, though I've never actually been there. A fitting place to write about socialist failures, don't you think? Do you have to go soon?"

I said I did. We shook hands and before I got to the door he was calling for another drink.

Now I owned a newspaper, such as it was; the next order of business was to find someone to run it. Back at the apartment I called Meyer Jaffe at his apartment hotel in New York. Meyer is an old time character actor who drifted into con games because there was more money in them, and he pulled off some beautiful scams before a five-year stretch in a French prison made him cautious. These days he works the safe side of the street; his last effort was the First Church of Elvis, which gains its inspiration from the life

44

and good works of the Blessed Presley. Meyer is many times an ordained minister, so what he does is legal if not honest. As an ordained minister he can ordain others at ten dollars a shot; you can find his boxed ad in the back pages of the supermarket scandal sheets. Through his ministry he gets Elvis to pray for you, to help you with your martial, financial, and personality problems, your feeling of inferiority. Business hasn't been as good as it was, because of the imitators now crowding the field, but as Meyers says, it's a living.

I met Meyer in the French slammer, at a time when I was being held for investigation of gun-running charges. After I was released for lack of evidence I sent Meyer some care packages to make the rest of his sentence a little easier. Since then I've used him, not very often, when I needed a front.

Meyer wasn't home and I left a call-back message.

The phone rang a few minutes later. "This is Rainey," I said.

"It certainly sounds like you," Meyer said. "Are you in Canada in business, or is it safer there than here?"

"Nothing like that, Meyer. You busy right now?"

"Never too busy if there's money in it. And provided it's not dangerous."

"No danger involved and I won't short you on the money. Come on up and we'll talk about it."

I gave him my address. There wasn't a lot to do after that. I read my Toronto guide book and studied the maps. My apartment was on Richmond Street West, on the other side of

York Street, it became Richmond Street East. I discovered where Union Station was and how to get there. O'Keefe Center, which had been built with O'Keefe's Beer money, was the equal of the Kennedy Center in Washington. The Parliament Buildings were in the south half of Queen's Park. Wellesley Street, which cut the park in two, ran from Queen's Park Crescent to Jarvis Street. After another week of this I'd be ready to go on a quiz show and give Toronto as my special subject.

Meyer arrived at six o'clock. A jaunty little guy at sixty-five, he dresses too young for his age, but he gets away with it because, as he says himself, he thinks young. His cord suit was unwrinkled, his blue oxford buttoned-down shirt unwilted in spite of the heat. I'm sure his striped tie had something to do with one of the Ivy League schools. For a guy that never got through high school, Meyer is a terrible snob and he says he wouldn't be caught dead in anything from Brooks Bros., preferring instead to buy his clothes at J. Press or Paul Stuart, whatever that is supposed to mean.

Meyer doesn't drink. I gave him coffee. He folded his jacket and put it over the back of a chair.

"So talk," he said.

I filled him in on what I was trying to do. "I want to have a real Canadian background when I go over there," I said. "The Russians will start checking me out as soon as I apply for the visa. How hard they'll check I don't know. If they check back to year one, then I'm in deep trouble. It wouldn't be so bad if they just said no. Then I'd have to do it some other way."

46

Meyer nodded. "You'd have a problem if they let you go to Vietnam knowing you were a phony. You'd be walking right into it."

"That's a chance I have to take."

"Why?"

"In my business you have to take chances. Albergo is paying top dollar."

"It's only money," Meyer said. "Would you listen to some sound advice from an old friend? Don't do it. It isn't worth it. No matter what the guinea is paying, it isn't worth it. Give him— send him—back every dollar you took from him. I'm surprised at you, doing business with mobsters."

"I made a deal, Meyer."

"Screw the deal! Go fight in some nice safe war."

"Enough," I said. "The deal is set. You want to hear the rest of it?"

Meyer heaved a breathy sigh. "I'm supposed to run this left-wing rag for you?"

"Yeah, I'm the publisher and editor-in-chief. You're the managing editor, the guy who puts everything together. Did you ever play an editor on or off the stage?"

Meyer searched his memory. "I had a bit part in a revival of *The Front Page*. That was summer theater, 1938. I can bone up on the part. No big deal."

"My background is, I've been writing stuff for the *Progressive World* for years. Lasker wrote the whole paper himself, using a whole slew of names. We'll choose one that looks important and that can be me. That's the pen name I'll give the Russians. At the same time I'll tell them I just bought the paper and will be publishing it from now on."

"But I'm an old employee," Meyer said. "Have been with the good old *Progressive* for donkey's years. When the Russians call, I'll say, 'Of course I know Mr. Stewart. He's our new proprietor and publisher and before he became the new boss he was one of our most valued contributors. You shoulda read his interesting series on union busting in the Hudson's Bay blubber factories.'"

"All right already," I said.

"I was just being facetious," Meyer said. "I know exactly what's expected of me." He pinched the razor-sharp crease in his trousers. "I'm going to need some new old clothes, a baggy pin-striped, double-breasted. Black shoes slightly cracked, certainly down at the heel. White socks, I think. I may grow a goatee. A lot of old-timey socialists had them: the mark of the intellectual. What do you think of the name Anton Steiner?"

"I leave all that to you," I said. "Just do it right. I don't want you getting too hammy."

Meyer raised his eyebrows. "Hammy! I don't know that I've ever been accused of that."

"Okay, we won't fight about it. Here are the keys to the office. I want you to hire a girl, a real dummy that knows how to type. Give her something to do to keep her busy. That's for if the Russians send a goon around. Oh yeah, get yourself a place to live, nothing fancy though. A residental hotel is probably the best. You're supposed to be one of life's losers, Meyer."

"Ah yes," Meyer said. "But a loser with principles. A man in his time plays many parts. This one, I must say, will be a novelty for me.

In the past I have been the Grand Duke Sergei, Mr. Cedric de Beers of the South African Diamond Exchange, Father Ettore Simonelli of the Vatican, and the homespun scientific genius, Dwight Henshaw, who perfected a dirt-cheap way of extracting gold from seawater. Now—what a comedown—I find myself a broken-down editorial hack with soup stains on his vest."

"You are hammy," I said, grinning at the mouthy little con man. "Now how much are your services going to cost me? Before you name a price, let me add that the paper belongs to you as soon as I get squared away. Maybe you could use it as part of some scam. I paid five thousand."

Meyer forgot that he had decided not to drink my instant coffee. He took a sip and made a face. "You got robbed, but I'll be glad to take it off your hands for nothing. There could be an angle there. Straight cash, I think I'm going to want a thousand a week for as long as it takes. Who's to say the KGB won't torture me? That ought to be worth a thousand a week."

Meyer wouldn't be Meyer if he didn't try to put his thumb on the scales. But he was an honest crook and I trusted him. "The KGB won't lay a hand on you and you know it." I counted out ten hundred dollar bills. "There's your first week. Better get on down to the office, Mr. Steiner. You don't want to docked for lateness."

Meyer got up and put on his jacket. "No fringe benefits, I suppose?"

"You can screw the typist is she lets you."

"Even if she lets me, I couldn't." Meyer put on his serious face, probably the face he used when he was Father Simonelli of the Vatican. "Rainey," he said, "you're going to a lot of trouble to set this up. That's as it should be. Details are what count, but you have to realize that anything can go wrong. Not a big thing. A little thing is all it takes and you'll be finished. That time before I got busted in France I thought not a thing could mess me up. Like you're doing now, I worked it out detail by detail. Like one of those creatures that build coral reefs, only I did it even better, spend a lot more time than you're doing."

"You told me all this in prison."

"It bears repeating, smart guy. I was working on this English widow so fucking old she went back to the Argentine tango craze that was hot just before the First World War. She was mad for gauchos, so I came on like the last of the gauchos. A bit old for the part I will admit, but compared to her I was a callow youth. Fifty-five I was then, looked a vigorous forty, could still get it up. My Spanish was and is good. I learned to tango like a son of a bitch. An old greaser left over from the tango period taught me pampas lore, all that shit. He tried to teach me how to throw the bola. That's the thing with three balls gauchos throw to knock down cows. I just couldn't learn to do it. Fuck it, I said, who throws the bola in Paris? The subject may come up, but the old crow probably won't ask for a demonstration. But she did, Rainey, she did. At a party at her house. She *insisted*. All I succeeded in doing was breaking a fucking window. She laughed it off, but the next morning two fraud squad detectives showed up at my hotel. You get the point?

"I get the point," I said patiently. "How can I not get it? If you threw the bola as well as you throw the bull, you'd never have gone to jail."

Meyer didn't appreciate my lame joke. "All I got was a prison term. You slip up and you've bought the farm."

"Beat it, Meyer," I said. "Call back when you find a hotel. I'll see you at the office."

There was no need to keep after Meyer; the little rascal knew how things were done and I wouldn't be surprised if he came up with a few neat touches of his own.

I needed a police press card, but I couldn't apply for it with nothing but a birth certificate for ID. Nobody carries around a birth certificate; the press card could wait until I got the passport and driver's license. After I got it I'd probably stop my coral reef building, as Meyer called it.

Lasker remained something of a problem; the man was a rummy; rummies do what rummies do. I had to find out if he'd gone to North Bay, or if he planned to go soon. I called his Toronto number and got no answer. Several calls and several hours later and still no answer. Then I called the press bar where he hung out and the guy who picked up got cranky when he heard what I wanted.

"This isn't an answering service, mister."

"Sorry, it's important."

"You're not a collection agency, are you?"

"No, I'm a friend."

"Didn't know he had any. Okay. Okay. He was in this morning. Said he was going on vacation. Was carrying a suitcase. If you see him, tell him he still hasn't settled his tab. A guy can take a vacation oughta be able to settle his tab."

Late that afternoon I went to the office and and found Meyer reading throught back issues of *Progressive World*. The only change I could see was the new two-pot Mr. Coffee sitting on a table beside the editor's desk. Meyer hadn't bought his baggy pin-stripe yet.

"I got some broads coming in day after tomorrow," he said, turning a yellowing page. "You want a dummy. You'll get a dummy. These socialists are pretty messy. I called a cleaning service. You want coffee, Mr. Stewart?"

"No thanks, Anton," I said.

Meyer patted a stack of dusty newspapers. "I've been working back from the latest edition and there's something by an Ian MacAllister in every one of them. Long pieces attacking police brutality, corruption in government, American control of Canadian business, CIA covert action in Nicaragua, acid rain that originates south of the border. This guy Lasker-MacAllister doesn't like Americans."

"Sounds good. MacAllister's my man."

Meyer took off his reading glasses and gave me a stern look. "You better take a stack of these home and read what you've written. I've been at it four hours and my mind is bent. This guy has got to be the dullest writer in history."

"Then I'm in for a real treat."

"Better do it. Remember me and the bola."

"Don't start that again. Have you thought up a new name for the paper?"

Meyer found a scratch pad on the littered desk. "What I have so far," he said, "is *Canadian Independent*, *Social Justice*, *Straight Talk*, and *Stewart's Weekly*. I like *Stewart's Weekly* because it seems to say what it is, whatever that may be. I see *Stewart's Weekly* as belonging to a forthright guy who wants the world to know who he is and what his opinions are. I see..."

"Sold to the man with the striped tie," I said. "No need to go on with the spiel. *Stewart's Weekly* it is."

"Now who's the hambone?"Meyer jeered. "Listen, Rainey, I think we'll have to suspend publication for a couple of weeks. I mean, who's going to write this shit?"

"Not me," I said. "You're the managing editor, pal. Get Father Simonelli to do a piece on activist priests in Central America. Ask around, visit the Press Box. That's the bar where Lasker hangs out. Buy some shit, but don't pay too much. Newspaper people are whores: they'll write anything that keeps them in drinking money. Payment will be on publication, right?"

"I always knew you were a cheap bastard," Meyer said.

Back at the apartment, I read Ian MacAllister's shrill articles until my eyes glazed over. The weekend dragged by. On Monday, the old broad from the motor vehicles department called and said my road test was scheduled for that afternoon.

"See I haven't forgotten you, Mr. Stewart," she cooed.

I passed the road test; the next day I got the passport. Things were starting to move. The police gave me no trouble with the press card. With all that ID in my pocket, I was beginning to feel *Canadian*.

The Canadians are a polite people, the Russians are not, and when I presented myself at the Soviet consulate, I was treated with the slant-eyed surliness that is second nature to the folks who shoot down unarmed civilian jetliners.

Trepassers will be executed, I thought, as some glum-looking Slav escorted me to the visa section.

There, I filled out a lenghty form and was questioned by a humorless young woman in a lesbian suit. Why did I want to go to the Republic of Vietnam? What were my views of the Vietnam War? Had I ever served in th Canadian armed forces? Why did I use the pen name Ian MacAllister instead of my own name? How soon would the first edition of the revamped newspaper appear?

It went on and on.

Yarmolinsky was the name on the plastic ID card clipped to the breast pocket of her coat. I thought it suited her. She was brisk, relentless, and unappealing. The old broad at the motor vehicles office was old and affected, but at least she had a spark of life.

"How soon will you let me know?" I asked.

"You will hear from us when your application has been processed, Mr. Stewart. You understand the Soviet Government is merely acting as the agent of the Socialist Republic of Vietnam, a free and independent state in the socialist family of nations."

"Then you can't give me even a rough date?"

"No, Mr. Stewart. I cannot. You will receive a letter in due time."

At the office, Meyer was reading one of the new typescripts. He said it was a general outline of the new Social-Democrat party in Britain.

"How did it go?" he asked.

"Now it's hurry up and wait," I said.

Ever the optimist, Meyer said, "There's still time to change your mind, Mr. Stewart."

"No way, Anton."

But I wasn't sure he didn't have the right idea.

FOUR

I TOOK a Quantas flight to Singapore two days after I got the visa. There, I changed over to Singapore Airlines and went on to Saigon, now called Ho Chi Minh City. It was hard to get used to the new name; to me, it would always be Saigon, that French-looking city of wide boulevards and outdoor cafes set down in the tropics. A beautiful, sinister city of great contrasts: opulence and poverty, tranquility and violence. The French expected to be there forever, and they built it to last. They left it when they saw they couldn't win. And so, twenty years later, did the Americans. Not many people from the Western countries go there now.

As the plane came in to land at Ton Son Nhut airport, I remembered that the first time I had seen Saigon was from the landing craft, one of many, that took us from the army transport ship anchored fifty miles downriver. It was a hot, wet day in the winter rainy season; the South China Sea was flat and pewter-colored, and the landing craft came down out of the mouth of the river to take us off.

56

Some of the men were still seasick, in spite of the glassy sea, and no one was cheerful. Through the rain it was possible to see the low, tree-lined shore, and when the landing craft started up into the river, there was the smell of rotting vegetation...

Now, coming in to land, I could see the city spread out below, the canals that linked it to the Mekong River, the bright shine of the river itself, a helicopter flying low over the tops of the houses. The airport, once the busiest in South East Asia, didn't look so busy now that the war was long over and foreign travel restricted. I knew it well, but I wasn't glad to see it.

The plane touched down. I followed the other passengers—most of them were Singapore Chinese—to the main terminal building. It was blistering hot after the frigid air-conditioning of the plane. There were wide cracks in the runway and everything had that rundown air you often see in Communist countries where maintenance is months or years behind degeneration.

In the terminal the air-conditioning was turned off or wasn't working. Women in drab uniforms were sweeping the floor, stooping to pick up cigarette butts that hadn't been smoked down to the filter. A loudspeaker told us to form a line; men in gray uniforms without insignia backed up the loudspeaker's orders with shouts of their own.

I was taking my place behind a fat Chinese with a briefcase when a young man in a dark uniform came up and said, "You are Mr. William Malcolm Stewart from Toronto, Canada?"

"Yes," I said.

Someone had watched me boarding the Qantas jet in Toronto.

"You will come with me," the Vietnamese said. "Your luggage will be attended to."

He walked stiffly ahead of me, very much aware of his own importance. Put a uniform on an Asian and he stops smiling. This Asian led the way to a door with a guard with an AK-47 standing in front of it. He went in and there was a middle-aged man behind a steel desk, a long cigarette dangling like a burning fuse from his lower lip. My guide told me to wait, then went out. I sat down on a folding chair.

I waited while the man behind the desk read to the bottom of a typewritten sheet. They do that to make you nervous. Finally, he looked up, favoring me with a brief, impersonal smile.

"Welcome to the Socialist Republic of Vietnam," he said, holding out his hand. "Your passport, Mr. Stewart."

I gave it to him. After he got through looking at it, and that took a while, he pushed a buzzer and a uniformed woman with a scarred face took the passport away without saying a word. There was no explanation; none was needed.

"I am Major Phuong," the political policeman said. He opened a drawer and took out a file folder; in it was the form I had completed at the Soviet consulate in Toronto. There were several typewritten sheets in the file. Behind the major, an enlarged photograph of Ho Chi Minh took up most of the wall. I sat there watched by Uncle Ho while the major read through my file with a fresh cigarette drooping from his lower lip, smoking without once touching the cigarette with his fingers.

"Now then" he said, looking up, "you must explain your reason for wanting to visit the Socialist Republic of Vietnam."

Later I was to learn that nowadays they are required to refer to the country in that way. You won't get jailed or shot if you simply say "Vietnam," but they like it better if you follow the correct usage.

"I thought I explained that in my application," I said.

"Explain it again—to me," the major said.

His English was very good, and I was sure he spoke other foreign languages. Here was a man who had been a Communist for most of his life. He might have started as a civil servant under the old French regime.

I didn't want to say too much; he had asked for an explanation not a point by point argument. My reason for wanting to see his country couldn't be made more important that it was.

"I've always been interested in Vietnam," I told him. "The Socialist Republic of Vietnam." I smiled but he didn't smile back. "There are other socialist countries I'd like to see, but your country interests me right now."

"Why?"

"Well, it's because Vietnam is the first socialist country to win its independence by winning a war against a major power. The Communist insurgents were defeated in the Greek civil war, in the campaign against the British in Malaya. They failed to take over Indonesia, didn't even come close in spite of their numbers. They say the Indonesians killed up to a million Communists. The figure may be inflated. Here, it was different: you won."

Major Phuong pasted another cigarette to his lip. "Yes, we won. Continue, Mr. Stewart."

"I don't know that I have much more to say, Major. What I mean is, your country did it the hard way. For instance, Castro fought well, but he was fighting a corrupt, disintegrating government. It would not have been so easy if the Americans had been backing Batista."

"The Americans supported Batista for years."

"But not with troops. The Americans put a million and a half men in here and still they lost. They call it a withdrawal, a disengagement, but it was a defeat. Losing here changed American politics, changed things all over the world. They lost face and they're still paying for it."

The major smiled. "So they invade little Grenada to show the world how mighty they are."

"That was part of Reagan's reelection campaign," I said. "Public relations. It took Americans back to the happier, simpler days of Teddy Roosevelt. Regan invaded Grenada because he saw how popular the Falklands war made Mrs. Thatcher."

"Yes, they like to try out their latest weapons on weak opponents. Are you anti-American, Mr. Stewart?"

"No more so than many Canadians," I said.

"But your sympathies are with the socialist countries?"

"I am interested in what they are doing," I told him. "The world has been going socialist since the end of the Second World War. It's a political reality that can't be ignored. What interests me is the difference between one socialist country and another. The Americans see them as a solid bloc...well, two solid blocs controlled by the Russians or the Chinese. I can't agree with that: there are national differences."

"For instance?" the major prompted.

"Well, everybody expected a bloodbath here after the Americans pulled out. It didn't happen. Even the Americans are forced to admit that. I suppose there were some executions, but nothing like the wholesale killing that followed Castro's take-over. From what I've read, many of doubtful loyalty were sent to reeducation camps. I don't doubt they were harshly treated. It was better than mass slaughter. That makes Vietnam different from, say, Cambodia. I think socialism has many faces."

"You don't mean masks?"

"No, I mean faces. No face tells everything, but it doesn't have to be a mask."

"Tell me," the major said, making no comment on what I'd said, "do you consider yourself a socialist?"

"In a general sense, yes. After all, capitalism is just one of the many political systems that have existed throughout history. The Americans like to believe it is most in tune with man's longing for personal freedom, his desire to own property. I'm inclined to disagree. I think there is nothing that can't be unlearned. Class warfare and wars of liberation may be necessary in the first stages of a revolution, but I would hope that in time social change can be brought about by education."

I hoped the major took me for a typical half-baked liberal. But all he did was grunt and go

61

back to my file.

"I see you walk with the aid of a cane," he said. "Have you been in military service?"

"No, I have a bad leg. An automobile accident some years ago. Anyway, there's no conscription in Canada."

"Then you have always been a journalist?"

"A free-lance journalist, yes. When I was young, I thought of trying for a job on a big newspaper, but gave up when I realized I'd have to write what I was told to write. You follow the rules or there's no place for you."

"You don't like to abide by the rules."

"If they make sense, I do."

Major Phuong closed my file and put it in the drawer. "Our rules for foreign visitors are very strict. Any serious deviation will result in your immediate expulsion. You will be accompanied by a guide at all times. For your own protection and for reasons of security. Where you can go, what you can see, will be at your guide's discretion. There can be no appeal from your guide's decisions. Another point of equal importance is this. The Socialist Republic of Vietnam has no diplomatic ties with Canada. Therefore, you cannot expect any help from your Government if an unpleasant incident should arise. The fact that Canada took no part in the American war of aggression against the people of the Socialist Republic of Vietnam is in your favor. But I would caution you not to attempt to take advantage of our goodwill."

"I had no such intention, Major."

Major Phuong waved that aside. "You have come here of your own free will. No one sent for you. Personally I see nothing to be gained by allowing foreign journalists to enter this country, but the decision to grant you a visa was not up to me. You will be under constant observation. It cannot be otherwise in a country that still faces many dangers from without. If all this does not suit your plans, then it would be advisable to take the next plane out."

"I wouldn't want to do that after coming so far. Major, I'll do nothing to make trouble. I'm not a rich man and won't get many opportunities for foreign travel. I've been looking forward to this for a long time."

The scarred woman came in with my passport and put it on the major's desk. Nothing was said. Major Phuong pushed the passport across the desk. I put it in my pocket.

"Very well then," the major said. "Your visa allows you to remain in the Socialist Republic of Vietnam for sixty days. For a longer stay, you must receive special permission. The Government is unlikely to grant it. Have you any questions? You may ask. I may not answer."

"A few questions. There have been persistent reports of anti-government guerrilla activity inside Vietnam. Is there any truth to it?"

The major squinted at me through a fog of cigarette smoke. It was a toss-up whether he'd die of lung cancer or lip cancer. Asians smoke as much as the booze-deprived rummies at AA meetings.

"Be more specific, Mr. Stewart."

"It's been said that certain guerrilla groups still operate with the backing of the Chinese. Cambodia is said to be involved because its government is allied to China. You are, in a way, caught between them. Neither government likes the Soviet influence here. My question is, do these guerrillas exist and are they a threat to your country?"

"There is no Soviet influence here and no guerrillas," the major said blandly. "What you are repeating is nothing more than American propaganda. Having failed to subjugate the peace-loving people of the Socialist Republic of Vietnam, the Americans now attempt to sow the seeds of dissent. They strive to exaggerate the small misunderstandings which sometimes occur between socialist countries with common borders. Such misunderstandings may result from a breakdown in communications or a wrongful interpretation of policy. They may even result from the fact that we speak different languages. Something may be lost in translation, as they say. But whatever these misunderstandings may be, we're all on the same side in the ongoing struggle against American imperialism."

All this was said with a straight face; the major couldn't have sounded more reasonable.

I dared to disagree. "Surely your invasion of Cambodia in Seventy-eight was more than a misunderstanding. After Pol Pot's forces were scattered you installed a new government in Phnom Penh. Your invasion force has been put at two hundred thousand men. In retaliation, the Chinese invaded the northern part of your country with a huge invasion force of their own. They stayed for a month and inflicted heavy damage on the northern industrial areas. That was January of Seventy-nine."

The major remained patient. "A misunderstanding," he repeated, bland as hospital food. I'd run into this Communist doublctalk before, but it still surprised me, the way they're able to carry it out without a trace of embarrassment. "You must not believe everything you read in the American press, Mr. Stewart. Reagan lied about Grenada, about Lebanon, about everything. Was there anything else you wanted to know?"

"Will you, will someone want to read my notes when I am ready to leave? Will what I write be censored?"

"I hardly think so," the major said. "How can you write about what you are not permitted to see? Are Canadian journalists permitted to wander through secret military installations? Of course not. As to your notes and other writings, what would be the point of censoring them when you carry the information in your head? However, I'm sure you will give a fair account of what you observe. And now..."

I stood up. "How soon do I get to meet my guide?"

"Later in the day," the major said. "For now, you will be escorted to your hotel. It's quite comfortable, I assure you. All our foreign visitors stay there. There will be no charge. You are the guest of the Socialist Republic of Vietnam."

The major pushed another button and the young officer in the dark uniform appeared.

"Take Mr. Stewart to his hotel," the major said.

I was going out the door when the major said, "You're not a foreign agent, are you, Mr. Stewart?"

I turned to look at him. "No, I'm not. If that's what you suspect, why are you letting me go?"

"I just thought I'd ask," the major said. "An

afterthought. An ocupational reflex. Disregard it. As to letting you go? I can let anyone go because I know they can't go far. I trust you will enjoy your stay among us. Your hotel, by the way, used to be called the Hilton."

The major was having his little joke; from the top of the Hilton, the ultimate symbol of American decadence, it used to be possible to watch our gunships rocketing VC positions far out on the delta. Americans, military and civilian, could get drunk while they had a ringside seat on the war. The Saigon Hilton was everything the VC believed they were fighting against. GI's, who couldn't afford it, hated it too.

I was driven there in a Russian Ziv, a small car that looks like a packing case on wheels. The big hotel looked as neglected as the airport. Going into town I had no trouble recognizing the streets, public buildings, other familiar landmarks. No signs of the war remained, and even in my time it hadn't suffered much damage because the VC had no air force, no planes of any kind. The streets were cleaner, less crowded than I remembered them, and in the faces of the people there was none of that almost hysterical gaiety that characterized the war years. Enormous pictures of Uncle Ho watched over the new order of things; the little Asian who had worked as a waiter in London had made it all possible.

At the front desk there was no need to register; it had been done for me. In the lobby, Chinese and other Asian businesmen stood around talking. A few of them had been with me on the flight from Singapore. China and Vietnam were on the outs, but it wasn't serious enough to get in the way of business. The desk clerk gaved my key to my guardian; he gave it to me.

"You will wait for your guide to arrive," he told me.

"Do I have to wait in my room? I'd like to walk around, get something to eat."

He consulted his rule book of a mind. "You need not stay in your room. But you must not leave the hotel. You may be approached to trade your Canadian or American dollars at a very favorable rate of exchange. Under no circumstance are you to do so. Illegal trade in foreign currency is a most serious offense."

I allowed myself some slight impatience. "Is that all you have to tell me?"

"No," he said, "there is something else. If you leave your room, you must inform the desk where you may be found by your guide."

Finding nothing else to warn me about, he stalked out to his car. I was glad to be rid of the officious son of a bitch; the political police have to be taken in small doses. What I wanted right then was a drink and some time to think, and I hoped my guide wouldn't turn up too soon. My guide, I felt sure, would be another pompous pain in the ass.

These days the Hilton is known as the July 2nd Hotel; that's the date the Socialist Republic of Vietnam was officially proclaimed in 1976. It doesn't have bellboys anymore; the carpets in the hallways have worn thin, with holes in places where traffic is heavy. It was cooler inside than out, which meant that the air-conditioning plant was fighting to the end.

I had a room on the tenth floor. It might have been bugged and probably was. The furniture was standard Hilton, but had seen better days, and there was the smell of red fish sauce I remembered so well and hated so much. Soldiers had been quartered there, though not lately; the stink of fish sauce lingered on.

The color TV set worked, so did the shower. I showered in tepid water, put on the same shirt, tried to get room service. There was no room service.

"For beer you buy it in the bar," the operator told me.

I didn't ask about food, figuring for food you bought it in the restaurant. Before I went back downstairs I called the operator, gave my name, and said I'd be in the bar or the restaurant in case my tour guide showed up.

"You must tell me exactly where you will be," the operator scolded. "In the bar? In the restaurant? You cannot be in both places at once."

They're like that in every Communist country I've been in. If they can make life difficult, they will. Obstacles are put in your way every way you turn. The smallest thing becomes a hassle. Ask the time of day and they want to know why you want to know.

"Can I get a drink in the restaurant?" I asked, resigning myself to the way things worked.

Yes, she said, I could get a drink in the restaurant.

"Then I'll be in the restaurant," I said. "After that I'll be back here."

Downstairs the restaurant was crowded with Chinamen; the few whites looked like they came from behind the Iron Curtain. The suits and the haircuts give them away, and sometimes so do the faces. All the waiters were old and so surly that even in New York they could give lessons in rudeness. The menu was a single mimeographed sheet well seasoned with soup and gravy stains. I ordered steak and was told they were out of it; ditto for several other items.

"You eat fish. There is plenty of fish," the waiter said, ready to shuffle off if I took too long to make up my mind.

"What about the chicken?" I asked.

"The Chinese may have eaten all the chicken," he told me. "I will see if they have."

He brought me the beer I ordered; there was a long wait for the chicken. One thing the Communists hadn't fucked up was the really good beer they make in Vietnam.

A Chinaman watched me while I drank the beer. He looked as Chinese as the hustling businessmen from Singapore, and he dressed as they did, but I knew he was no commercial hustler, no ten-percenter. Where the Singapore Chinese were loud and gregarious this guy was quiet-looking and very deliberate in his movements; his eyes were calm and watchful.

I ignored him; being watched was something I'd have to get used to. He might drop out of sight as soon as my guide took me in tow, but there was always the possibility that he had been sent to watch both of us. People shadowing people is as much a part of life as underarm deodorant is not in the Communist countries. I knew what he looked like and that would make it easier to lose him when the time came to make my break.

My curried chicken finally arrived and it wasn't too bad for what it was. But I'd eaten better curried chicken on West 47th Street in New York. All the Chinese spook was having was tea. Maybe that was all the budget allowed. I passed up the dessert and drank another beer.

I was about to leave when the telephone operator paged me on the PA system. "Mr. William Stewart, go immediately to your room. Your official guide has arrived."

The message was repeated several times before I got to the elevators. While I was waiting the Chinaman came out of the restaurant and stood looking at a bulletin board. He didn't get on with me, but I guess he watched the indicator lights.

I thought it was pretty ballsy of the guide to go into my room instead of meeting me in the lobby. But after I opened the door—it wasn't locked—all my annoyance faded away.

FIVE

SHE WASN'T the most beautful woman I'd ever seen, but she was young and good-looking. I don't know why I was so surprised my guide was a woman. Most of the Intourist guides in the Soviet Union are women, some of them good-looking in their way; even so, I was surprised.

"Hello there," she said in an American accent, and that surprised me even more. "I'm Kim Anh Diem, your guide. You weren't here, so the floor warden let me in. That's how we live now in the Socialist Republic of Vietnam. No locked doors, no secrets. Privacy is an anti-social concept. Welcome to my country, Mr. Stewart."

My suitcase was in the closet; I wondered if she'd searched it. This Kim Anh Diem wore a well-tailored tan uniform of a kind I hadn't seen before. Maybe they made them specially for guides. She was slender, like most Vietnamese women, but there was enough of her to fill out the uniform. Her eyes had been fixed, meaning there had been plastic surgery to give her a more Western appearance. It would have been impolite to ask how that came about in an American-hating socialist republic.

"Well, what would you like to do first?" she asked.

"You speak very good English," I said.

"Why not? I went to Georgetown, where good Catholic girls go. Even good Vietnamese Catholic girls. I might as well explain so you won't keep on staring at me."

"I guess I was staring."

"That's okay. Most foreign visitors do. I don't explain to the ones I don't like. My father was a remote cousin of President Diem. Lucky for him it wasn't a close relationship or he wouldn't have survived the coup. But, you know, it was like being one of the Lees of Virginia. The Diem family tree isn't just any old tree. It's a great spreading oak with many branches. I think even the leaves mean something. My father was very proud to be a part of it, but he kept a low profile at the time of the coup. A smart man, my father, he knew the South was going to lose, so he got out, went to the States a year before it all came crashing down. Ten years ago, a long time. The whole family got out. A very rich family. My father was a rich man before the war. He got richer during it. What good is a war if you don't make money, right?"

That was a rhetorical question.

"We settled in Washington, a townhouse in Georgetown. A lovely federal house. Wide floorboards, a chaste brass knocker on the door, a narrow back staircase for the servants. My father was sure the South was going to lose, but he wanted to cover himself if it worked a miracle and won. He hired a PR man and let it

72

be known that he had come to Washington for surgery that couldn't be done at home. Didn't sound too unlikely. He was a frail, elderly man and his health had never been good. Well, you know, his phony operation wasn't a complete success and—what else?—he'd have to go back for a little corrective cutting from time to time. Of course, he'd have to stay in Washington for that. But even while he waited for the surgeon's scalpel, he continued to fight the good fight against godless Communism. Dirty Commie rats, did he hate 'em! All that bullshit clouded the fact that he'd run out on his own government. Didn't do him one bit of harm. The fascists here in Saigon probably figured they'd need him if they had to run. They even sent him a lot of money to add to his war graft. Money is all that counts in America. Doesn't matter where you get it. Who cares if it's been squeezed out of millions of people who are starving to death? The rest of my family didn't care. I cared."

"That's how you became a Communist?" Like all leftist zealots she had a fondness for the monologue. Actually it was more of a harangue. I felt I had to say something.

"Damn right it was. Funny thing, I had absolutely no interest in politics when I first went to the States. Nothing strange about that, a fifteen-year-old kid. I was pretty Americanized even before I got there. Of course, being Frenchified was the 'in' thing with the upper classes before the Americans came. A lot of older people stuck to that because they'd grown up under it, had gone to French schools, spoke French like the natives. Natives

73

of France, that is. The young people, kids like me, got turned on by these new strange Americans. Became acculturated, as they say. American culture my ass! What culture? But we went with it, the whole bit. Chewed gum, traded Elvis records, agreed that all the old Vietnamese ways were a fucking drag."

"The war brought many unfortunate changes," I said, lamenting the death of an ancient civilization. I had a beard and a cane and horn-rimmed glasses, so it was all right to say things like that. William Malcolm Stewart was nothing if not serious.

"You see these eyes of mine?" she said. "Getting round eyes was the biggest in thing to do. A few rich women did it, but mostly it was the whores. They thought they'd get a better price if they had round eyes. Stupid cunts, how could they know it was the exotic look the Americans were after? I should talk! I was just as dumb and all I can say is I was a kid."

"You can't have it changed back? I mean, if it bothers you so much."

It was an odd conversation to be having with a woman who was certainly a secret police agent. There was some French blood in her and with the light skin and the round eyes she could have passed for Italian or Spanish, most anything at all.

"I've thought about it," she said. "I'm not sure it's worth the bother. I've had these eyes since I was fourteen. I told my father I wanted to have it done and he was horrified. No way, he said. He was adamant about it. He sucked up to the Americans, but a round-eyed daughter was a no-no. A betrayal of our thousand-year

74

heritage and all that jazz. Daughter, you can't do that, he said. What will the nuns think? Fucking nuns! So what did I do? I ran away to Cholon—that's the Chinese section—and had it done by an outlaw Chink plastic surgeon with a big whore trade. Two weeks later I came back with my new eyes and my father nearly dropped dead. I had brought disgrace to the family, me and my hooker eyes. But, you know, there was nothing he could do about it."

It was a curious situation; I had no idea how she expected me to respond. As a Communist party member—she had to be, to get the job she had—she had to know about hotel rooms being bugged. More than likely she was an expert on the subject. Which meant there had to be a good reason why she was telling me her goddamned life story. It could be that she was laying groundwork for a recruitment attempt. That, or she was trying to get me to say things that could be used against me later.

"You look worried," she said.

"I'm not worried, Miss Diem."

That got a laugh. "Please, Mr. Stewart. Call me Comrade Diem or just Kim. Normally I'm referred to as Comrade Diem, but that's within the party. Foreign visitors aren't expected to conform so closely. For most Westerners the word comrade conjures up all sorts of authoritarian images. Plain bulky women in padded coats."

"With you that would be a mistake."

She accepted my little compliment with a smile and a nod. This guy William Malcolm Stewart might be serious as an owl, but he knew a good-looking broad when he saw one.

"I think you'd better call me Kim," she decided. "What are you called? Is it William or Bill?"

"Usually William."

"William suits you."

I hoped she wasn't going to come up close and look into my phony brown eyes. My soft contact lenses were the best money could buy, but they might not stand up under close scrutiny.

"There's no need to look so worried. Your room isn't bugged if that's what you're thinking. You know how many rooms there are in this hotel? I'll tell you. Seven hundred and two. Think of the expense, William. As a country we're not even a decade old. We put our money where it's needed, not in bugging the hotel rooms of sincere-looking Canadian journalists."

"That's good to hear. Bugging me would be a waste of time. I'm the most peaceful of all the peaced-loving people of Canada."

Another penetrating look followed that statement. "I'm not so sure you're as mild-mannered as you let on. But how would I know right? Hey, you want proof this room isn't bugged?"

I said I'd take her word for it.

"No, seriously," she said, "I'd like you to relax and enjoy your stay. You can't do that if you think there's a bug hidden in the light fixture or behind the picture of Uncle Ho. I'll show you."

She raised her voice and said, "Ho Chi Minh was a dirty old man, a defiler of little boys. Ho Chi Minh was a pervert and a shiteater. Ho Chi

76

Minh was a thief and a liar and a traitor to the revolution. I say this because I am a special agent of the CIA . . ."

She couldn't go on because she was laughing so hard. "If this room is bugged, you can expect me to be arrested in about three minutes. Except I won't be. Now are you convinced?"

"One hundred percent," I said, absolutely sure that the room was bugged. I was just as certain that this broad was no ordinary agent. Only someone special could get away with putting the bad-mouth on Uncle Ho. And there might come a time when it would stand her in front of a firing squad.

"Then relax," she said. "Where was I when you started to get worried?"

"Where you had your eyes fixed. You mind if I ask a question?"

"Ask anything you like, William."

"A lot of what you've been telling me is personal. Why would you want me to know?"

"Oh, I thought you understood. I was hoping you'd want to write about me. Don't get the wrong idea; there's no personal vanity involved. The party approves or I wouldn't have told you in such detail. Usually I give visitors a paragraph or two and let it go at that."

"The party approves?" I said.

"Yes, the party—the government, same thing—wants our young people to come home. To leave America or wherever they are and join the great work of building a socialist state that will set an example for the whole world. Ten years after the war there are thousands of college-educated Vietnamese young people in foreign countries. They don't belong there, they belong here. I was one of them and I came back. But, you know, being a Diem I had to pay my dues, and I don't mean to the party. I had to prove myself in every possible way."

"How?"

"I joined the party my second year in college. But I didn't jump in just like that. It had been coming for a long time. The more I saw of America, the more I saw how rotten it was. I saw a society that was built on greed and hypocrisy. All the shitty things I liked as a kid now made me want to throw up. But I was smart enough to keep my opinions to myself. My father would've had a fit if he knew the direction I was going. I rediscovered what it meant to be Vietnamese. I suppose I don't look much like a Viet with these fucking round eyes. But I am. God damn it, I am. Funny thing, I was living under the same roof as my father and he was CIA-connected and I was a member of the party. One thing you should remember when you write about me, if you do. Don't describe me as a card-carrying member of the party. We don't carry cards anymore, haven't for years."

I nodded. "I'm surprised the party didn't want you to stay in the States, become an agent."

"They did. I wanted to come back, but they ordered me to stay. I did some useful work, mostly spying on my father and his CIA contacts. I went to parties given by Vietnamese fascists in Washington, listened, and reported what I heard. I got around."

"Then why didn't you stay?"

"I got word the CIA was investigating me. I didn't want to wind up in a private hospital pumped full of truth drugs. I went to my control in Washington and he agreed it was time for me to get out. I did."

"Did you ever become a U.S. citizen?"

"My father did. I was a minor, so I did too. I wanted to give it up when I left the country. The party ordered me not to. So I have dual citizenship, Vietnamese and American."

"There's certainly a story there," I said.

"The party thinks so. They didn't always think that way. Now they do. If you write about me, forget about the *me*. I'm not interested in personal publicity. I'm twenty-five now and all that American PR crap is behind me. I'd like you to write the no-frills story of how one Vietnamese woman found her way back to her roots. How she found something useful to do with her life instead of ending up married to some money-chasing jerk in some fucking suburb."

"A communist inspirational?"

That made her eyes snap with defiance. "Call it what you like, William. I've learned not to be cynical. That's what it means to give yourself to a cause. When you discover something more important than yourself all the rubbishy things you used to clutter up your mind with no longer have meaning. Do you understand what I'm saying?"

"Yes, I think I do."

Looking at this broad I decided the stage had lost a great actor when she turned Red. There was so much sincerity in her face, in her voice, that if I hadn't been such a hard-assed old bastard I might have believed her. She was one lying, scheming, foxy lady! The guys who read her reports, listened to her taped performances, must have clucked their tongues in appreciation of her ability to throw the bull and make it sound like the sweetest truth. I wondered if she carried a gun in that leather bag slung from her shoulder. If she did—of course she did—it was sure to have a silencer attached. Was there a bullet in it for me? If there was, she wouldn't hesitate to put it in the back of my head.

"I hope I haven't bored you," she said.

"Not a bit," I answered truthfully. "I ought to tell you you're not what I expected a guide to be. What I thought I'd draw was one of your bulky women in padded coats. I'm agreeably surprised."

"Don't be so formal, William. Listen to me. I'd be a liar if I said I hadn't seen your file. Nothing sinister in that. A guide has to know what her visitors are like. What better way to find out? Saves time. But the file. It says you've never visited any of the other socialist countries."

I pulled at my beard, one of the moves I'd worked out. My beard and my cane were turning me into a character actor. Meyer Jaffe would have jeered if he'd been there to see it.

"Never could afford it," I told Comrade Kim. "I hate to admit it, but this is my first time out of Canada."

"Then you've probably come with a lot of preconceived notions about what socialism is like. My advice is, forget everything you've read, put it over the side, get rid of it. I know socialism is usually pictured as a drab colorless thing. Believe me, there's no truth in it. Of course, as you travel around this country with me, you won't find the consumer junk you're accustomed to in Canada. Color TV's, home computers, cordless telephones, Ken and Barbie dolls, self-cleaning ovens, the Avon Lady—you won't find any of that. You'll get used to it, though there may be some withdrawal symptoms in the beginning. Forge ahead, be of good cheer. After a while you'll begin to see things you never saw before. Really see! What you'll see, if you approach things with an open mind, is free, peace-loving people working hard to make socialist prosperity a reality. But, you know, it isn't all work and no play. We have good times here, simple good times, an enjoyment and appreciation of life that doesn't cost money."

"That I'd like to see."

"But you will," Comrade Kim said, bright-eyed as only a complete phony can be. Maybe that wasn't the right word for her; an agent doing a job wasn't a phony in the ordinary sense. Truth to tell, I couldn't decide what she was.

"What happens next?" I asked her.

"What would you like to happen?" she said. "Oh, I didn't mean it to sound like that. Perhaps it will happen, perhaps not. In spite of what you've heard about socialist puritanism we have a freer attitude here. During the war our fighting men and women slept together. They shared their bodies as they shared everything else. Sex became an act of love and friendship. There was no exploitation, no role playing,

81

none of that dreadful *using* you find in the capitalist countries, especially the United States. I'm glad you're not an American, William. There are some good Americans, of course, but you know what they say—feelings are facts. I think we are going to be wonderful friends."

"I'd like that," I said, wondering if I'd have to kill her when it was time to cut loose. I knew we'd end up in the sack, and that was fine with me, but I didn't look forward to screwing a broad one day and killing her the next. When all's said and done, there is such a thing as chivalry. Sure there is, and it can get you killed.

"Unless you're in a hurry to get started it's probably better if we wait till morning. Anyway, you haven't seen the city by night."

"I haven't seen it anytime."

"It's very different by night," she said. "Naturally it's quieter than during the war. It was so weird then, so surreal, if you know what I mean. There were always explosions at night. Bombing, artillery, mortars. Machine guns and automatic rifle fire. Gunships firing rockets. All going on right outside the city, in the suburbs. It went on during the day, but you noticed it more at night. Sometimes it got quiet for a few hours, but hardly ever. Imagine? I used to get mad at the Viet Cong because all the bombing interfered with TV reception. What a little idiot I was then! Why are you smiling?"

"I was just thinking you've come a long way from trading Elvis records," I said. I had been thinking that. It was the truth: she had left Elvis far behind.

She grew serious, or pretended to. "I have, haven't I? Oh, it's great, William, to find something you really put your heart into. Some of the girls I grew up with are still here." She laughed with self-satisfied contempt. "Not all the rich families got out with the Americans. They hung on hoping for a sign from heaven. It didn't come—and was that a shock! These girls I used to know, I still see one or two of them by accident. They're not so complacent now. Just last week I was taking Swedish visitors on a tour of a socialist seamen's hotel down by the river and one of them was working in the kitchen. Oh how the mighty have fallen! This girl's father used to be one of the wealthiest men in the country."

"Well, she won't starve in the kitchen," I said.

"Nobody starves in our new society," Comrade Kim stated. "My one-time friend is doing useful work and there may be hope for her yet. We don't kill people unless we have to. We try to show them that their reactionary attitudes are as harmful to themselves as they are to society. Sorry, no more lectures for now. I get carried away. Let's go out and see the city. You'll like it. No bombs or bullets these days. Dine without danger, right?"

I decided to give her a little test. "Something slipped my mind, we were talking so much."

"Okay, I was talking too much. What is it?"

"A man was watching me in the restaurant today. Just before I came up here. A Chinese. He watched me all the time I was eating. I don't think I'm mistaken."

Comrade Kim smiled. "Of course he was watching you. Your clothes are American, you look American. Okay, Canadian. Same thing. How many Americans do you think this Chinese sees in Ho Chi Minh City? You must have looked like the Man from Mars to him."

I showed the stubborn Scots side of William Stewart's nature. "I see what you mean, but why did he keep on watching me after all the others had stopped? From the others I just got curious looks, that was all. This man ordered nothing but tea and took an awfully long time to drink it. Another thing: all the other Chinese were in groups. This man was by himself."

Her smile stayed in place though it looked a little fixed. "A solitary tea drinker! He was alone, had no one to talk to, so he stared at you. What's so unusual about that?"

"He didn't stare."

"Okay, he didn't stare."

"And he got up when I did. And he followed me out to the elevators. I had to wait for the elevator. He pretended to be looking at a bulletin board. Usually I'm not too observant, but there was no way I could miss what he was doing. He was watching me."

Her smile wasn't so natural now. "You're sure about this?"

"I'm sure. Major Phuong warned me to steer clear of illegal currency dealers. You think he could have been and couldn't get up the nerve to approach me?"

"Those parasites have plenty of nerve," Comrade Kim said, no longer warming me with her smile.

I pressed on. "Could he have been one of Major Phuong's men? The major did warn me that I'd be under observation."

This time she frowned. "You wouldn't see Major Phuong's men if they wanted to watch you. It's probably nothing. But if it bothers you I think I ought to make a phone call."

That's what she said, but something told me she was more bothered than I was; something like inner agitation showed through as she told the operator to give her an outside line. I figured that's what she said. I don't speak Vietnamese.

This customer was always right; the snotty operator gave her no back talk. She dialed, waited, asked for Major Phuong. I caught the name Phuong. Then there was a short conversation, none of which I understood. She hung up.

"Forget it," she said. Major Phuong isn't having you watched." Her laugh was forced. "He tells that to all foreign visitors. Who knows what your Chinese admirer was up to? Perhaps you're right and he was a dirty little money-changer. The hell with him, whoever he was. Let's go and get a drink. My job is one job where you can drink on duty. Have to keep our visitors happy, you know."

We went down in the elevator and Comrade Kim was smiling again, There was no sign of her earlier concern.

"Isn't this more interesting than Toronto?" she said

I wondered where the Chinaman was.

SIX

I DIDN'T have to wait long to find out.

We were coming out of the hotel. It was getting dark and there were a few taxis out front letting off passengers. Taxis waiting for fares were in a short line to the left. Comrade Kim was saying something; I was looking for the Chinaman. Suddenly an engine roared and a taxi not in the line came tearing down the street with its high beams on. It swerved over toward us and then I saw the Chinaman sticking an M-16 out through the back window.

"Get down!" I yelled at Kim, shoving her to one side. The M-16 rattled bullets at us. People behind us were cut down by the blast and Kim was pulling an automatic pistol from her shoulder bag when a lurching body hit her and knocked her down. The automatic went skittering on the concrete and I dived for it while the taxi began to back up so the Chinaman could get a better shot at us. One of the taxis pulled out of the line and got in his way and caught a lot of lead before it went past and jumped the curb. The taxi with the

Chinaman in it was still backing up. I could see the Chinaman's face over the top of the rifle. I gave the Chinaman and the taxi most of the clip. He took some bullets in the face and the M-16 fell out the window. I fired at the taxi. It swerved sideways and was struck by a van that tried to get out of its way. The collision killed the motor and the starter clattered as the driver tried to get it started again. Then the driver jumped out bloody-faced and staggering and ran into the parking lot and disappeared.

I pulled Kim to her feet. She was dazed and I had to steady her. People were running in and out of the hotel; a police jeep with two men in it pulled up with a screech of tires. They jumped out and menaced everyone with their submachine guns. Dead and wounded were on the steps and the sidewalk, and there was a lot of blood. A woman was on her knees, feeling her body with her hands and sobbing. I couldn't see any holes in her. Kim looked at the gun in my hand, at the dead Chinaman hanging out the window of the wrecked taxi. Then she waved the police submachine guns away from us, holding out her ID in a leather case.

The two cops jerked to attention and saluted. Kim rattled off orders in Vietnamese. One of the cops went to the jeep and talked on the radio. The other cop pulled the dead Chinaman out of the taxi. We went over and looked at him. Two more police jeeps were pulling in.

The Chinaman lay on his back, three holes in his face, blood all over his tropical suit. Even with his new face I knew it was the same guy. The cop who used the radio was holding the

87

killer's rifle. Kneeling beside the corpse, the other cop was looking for ID. He straightened, shrugged, and said something to Kim.

"Nothing to identify him", Kim said to me, holding out her hand to take back her pistol. It had a silencer on it. She pushed in a fresh clip before she put it in her bag.

"You saved my life," she said. Her eyes went back to the holes in the Chinaman's face. "You're a good shot, for a journalist."

"I just pointed and kept pulling the trigger. He was close enough, I had to hit something. There wasn't time to think about it. My God, I killed a man I didn't even know."

Kim looked at the corpse. "You killed him, all right."

I turned the other way and so did she. My explanation about the hit and miss shooting didn't get much of a reaction out of her.

"Which of us do you think he was shooting at?" I said. "It must have been me. Unless he knew you were coming to meet me, then it must hae been me."

Kim straightened the strap of her shoulder bag. There was dirt on her uniform and she rubbed at it; the shooting had rattled her more than she let on.

"It's all some weird misunderstanding," she said. Misunderstanding? Major Phuong had used the same word. A catch-all to cover any situation. "He may have been insane, some crazy drug addict out to kill somebody. You'll see. An autopsy is sure to turn up drugs."

A wrecker came to tow the taxi away. Two ambulances arrived, one for the dead, one for the wounded. The taxi driver who got in the way of the Chinaman's M-16 was dead. He was the last to be loaded. Now the street was clear and there was nothing more to gape at; people drifted away.

"Maybe crazy or he was on drugs," I said. "But how does that explain the taxi and the man who drove him? Nuts usually do these things on their own. How do you explain the other man?"

"I don't explain him. That's up to the police," She sounded edgy. "The dead man may have lost his family in the war. An American bombing raid, perhaps. You could be American. I don't know. It's possible he was shooting at one of the people behind us. They're all dead or wounded and we're not."

"They didn't duck fast enough."

"Let it go. We may never know what was in his crazy mind. Come on, we have to see Major Phuong."

"At the airport?"

Kim was patient with me. "Not at the airport, William. Major Phuong's authority extends far beyond the airport."

As if I didn't know.

A taxi took us to the old French Surete building, a grim old pile of stone on Fidel Castro Street. I couldn't recall what the original French name had been. It had been heavily sandbagged during the war. Now the sandbags and the barbed wire were gone. An armored car was parked in front of the main entrance. Kim showed her ID to a guard and we went up a flight of stairs to Major Phuong's office.

We weren't there very long. Kim and the major talked in Vietnamese. I leaned on my cane and looked suitably shaken by the terrible experience I'd been through. Now and then the major looked at me.

The office needed a paint job; the furniture was old and battered; the whole place smelled of fear. A small copper-plated kettle hissed on a spirit lamp. A long cigarette smoldered in an ashtray while the major nibbled at sticky-looking pastry. He finished eating and put the cigarette in his mouth.

Now it was my turn.

"Comrade Diem has made a full report," he said in English. "I wish to offer my most sincere apologies on behalf of the Socialist Republic of Vietnam. A regrettable incident, to be sure. You say this assassin watched you while you were dining?"

"I'm sure of it, Major."

"Well then, we must accept the fact that he did. Some fanatic, no doubt. A drug-crazed maniac for all his quiet appearance. Of course you'd never seen him before?"

"Absolutely not," I said.

The major nodded; his face was closed and bland. He leaned over to turn down the flame of the alcohol lamp. Then he spooned tea into a teapot decorated with dragons.

"A misunderstanding," he said, pouring hot water into the pot. "I can't imagine what else it can be. Nothing much can be learned until the dead man's fingerprints have been taken, his face compared with our photographic files."

I did some nodding of my own.

Major Phuong put the lid on the teapot. "The assassin's face," he said. "Comrade Diem says you shot him three times in the face. What luck! To hit him three times in a moving taxi!"

I took no credit for marksmanship. "I was scared to death," I said. "Kill or be killed. I grabbed Miss Diem's revolver and blazed away."

"Comrade Diem's firearm is an automatic pistol, not a revolver. But you can hardly be expected to know the difference."

"I feel sick about it," I said, passing over the technical talk. "My first day in your country and I end up killing another human being. It hardly seems possible."

The major offered me tea.

"I'm sorry. Tea is all I have," he said when I turned it down. "Yes, it must have been a terrible shock for you. You must calm yourself and try to put it out of your mind."

I pulled at my beard. It was okay to look nervous. "I'll try, Major, but it won't be easy with that other man—the driver—on the loose."

Major Phuong sipped his tea. "We'll find him, Mr. Stewart. We'll know all about this once we find him."

I began to feel sorry for the guy, wherever he was.

I was ready to call it a night, but Kim wanted me to see Saigon after dark. As if I hadn't seen Saigon at all times, in all seasons. Not all my work as part of the Phoenix Group hit team had been done in the boondocks. One hit had been done just like my dead Chinaman's, from a moving taxi; the target was an ARVN—South Vietnamese Army—colonel who'd been selling weapons to the VC. We had to do it that way because he was splitting the loot with high muckymucks in the government and couldn't be got at through channels. There had been other hits, not all of them after dark.

"We could use an official car," Kim said. "But I don't think you want that."

"I could do without it."

"It won't bother you to walk?"

That was out of concern for my game leg. "Exercise does me good. I've had enough taxis for one night."

"So have I. But there won't be any more of that."

I don't know how she knew. She couldn't have. It was meant to reassure. But she was right. Hits hardly ever come in pairs. If one doesn't work, you try another. That takes time unless it's a hit that can't wait. I figured they could plan the next attempt a little more carefully.

We ate in an Armenian restaurant near the Cathedral. I guess they were Soviet Armenians. Walking there we passed many girls in white trousers on bicycles; the few cars in the streets had official markings. For a city without sin, Saigon still had plenty of whores. But they didn't strut and they didn't yell and they took off fast when they saw Kim's uniform.

There was twangy music to go with the food. I don't know why Kim chose an Armenian place. Home cooking would have seemed more in order. Maybe the joint was run by Armenian KGB agents and she felt safer there. We had roast lamb and yellow rice. I had beer, Kim had something with rum in it. The place got a mixed bag of Vietnamese, Chinese, a few Warsaw Pact types with bad haircuts.

"I suppose you're wondering about the gun," Kim said, sipping her drink.

"Not really. I'm just glad you had it. We wouldn't be here now if you hadn't."

"You probably think I'm a police agent."

"I suppose that's the way the system works."

"I report to the political police," Kim said. "There's a difference. But I'm not a police agent. I'm here as a guide not as a spy. The gun . . . well, the gun is for the protection of my guests. I've carried it since I starterd this job and never had to use it before. Correction: this is the first time it had to be used. I'm afraid I'm not much of a bodyguard. That ought to prove I'm no trained agent. A real agent would've been quicker."

"In the movies they're very quick," I said.

There was a sort of shrine to Ho Chi Minh in the back of the room. Uncle Ho's crinkly eyes watched me through flickering candlelight. I knew he had me pegged for a counterfeit.

Kim laughed in that birdlike way Vietnamese women have. Even Georgetown hadn't been able to change that. But in every other way she was as Americanized as Charlie Chan's No.1 Son, the guy who kept saying "Gee Willickers, Pop!"

"Seriously though," she said, "I have to carry the gun. All the guides do. I wish I didn't. The way I handled myself won't look so great on my record."

"You can't take the credit? The way police back home do it when they want some guy to look good?"

"Not here."

"Will it be in the papers? I wouldn't like it if the Canadian papers picked it up."

"Why? It couldn't do your career any harm.

Think of the publicity. How many newsmen come that close to the news?"

"I'm not that kind of newsman. I still can't believe what happened tonight. All the people he killed . . . and then I killed him. I keep seeing the look on his faced as he fired the machine gun. No, that isn't right. His face was blank, no expression at all."

"An American M-16 automatic rifle," Kim said. "Not a machine gun. You should get it right if you're going to write about it. Before the M-16 there was an M-15. The Americans are always perfecting new ways of killing people."

"Thanks for the lesson," I said. "But I have no interest in guns of any kind. The world would be better off without them."

"Tell that to the Americans."

"And the Russians."

Kim frowned. "The socialist countries have to defend thenselves. Oh well. Let's not get into a political discussion. You haven't been here long enough for that. If you're still worrying about the newspapers—don't. There won't be a word about it in tomorrow's paper. Why encourage other madmen to commit antisocial acts?"

I liked the way she described mass murder; people who specialize tend to talk in jargon. Once I asked a steely-eyed feminist if "hangperson" was the correct, nonsexist word for an executioner who worked with a rope. She didn't think it was funny. I decided not to try any of that stuff with Kim. More of interest to me was the silencer attached to her automatic pistol. A silencer is not a defense feature of firearms. Killers use silencers,

94

therefore...

"Don't you ever drink anything stronger than beer?" Kim asked, flagging down the waiter with her empty glass.

"Hardly ever," I said. "Hard liquor knocks me out too fast. I like to know what I'm doing."

Kim got her rum drink, I had some beer left. Two policemen came in asking to see passports and ID papers. They gave the Chinese a hard time. Kim waved them away from our table with her ID card. One quick look at the card and they beat it.

"You're too much on the defensive," Kim said. "You must learn to trust people. You drink beer because you're afraid to let yourself go. Don't you know there's no such thing as being completely safe?"

Maybe there was rum in her drink. I couldn't be sure. She was beginning to sound like there was. But that could have been part of her act. This broad had more moves than a one-man band.

"I guess I've led a sheltered life."

"Too sheltered, it seems to me. And yet, deep down, there seems to be a reckless core to your nature. Am I wrong.?"

She talked that way—part Marxist jargon, part soap opera. Her drink was half gone and she was bright-eyed. That didn't prove there was rum in her drink. Some actresses can cry on cue. This one was Oscar material.

"You're wrong," I said. "My idea of being reckless is buying *two* raffle tickets."

The twangy music was on a tape. It went back to the beginning. Catchy stuff, probably top of the charts in Soviet Armenia. The

Warsaw Pact types paid their bill and left.

"I don't believe you," Kim said. "What do you do with yourself back in Toronto? I've been in Canada many times."

Here it comes, I thought. Her best friend at Georgetown came from Toronto. She spent a whole summer there and knows the city like a book.

"How did you like it?" I said cautiously.

"Skiing in the Laurentians was the extent of my travels. That and a few stopovers in Montreal. That was before I went to college. You didn't answer the question. How do you spend your time when you aren't writing?"

"I keep busy enough. Reading. Movies. My main interest is politics. The Canadian provinces aren't like the American states. The federal alliance is looser and much more recent. No matter what Trudeau says, Quebec may declare for independence one of these days. It may go completely socialist when it does. I can't see Trudeau invading the province with federal forces."

"No, he'll get Reagan to do it for him. Too bad Quebec doesn't have a medical school chockful of Americans. That would give the Yankee cowboy a good excuse. Not that the son of a bitch need an excuse to do anything."

She went on and on with her denunciation of Reagan. She quoted Marx, Lenin, Tip O'Neill. I didn't think it was fair to put Tip in such bad company. Somewhere along the line she asked if I'd ever considered becoming a Communist.

"When I was young," I answered. "It's something you think about when you're young. I was close to joining when the Russians invaded Hungary in Fifty-six. That turned me off."

"The Hungarian uprising was a fascist plot," Kim said.

"So I've heard."

"It's true. The CIA tried to unite every fascist and reactionary group in Hungary. America might have intervened if the Soviets hadn't acted swiftly."

A not-so-brief lecture followed. Pressed to the wall, I was ready to admit that the Americans had incited the Hungarians to rebellion, then left them in the lurch.

Kim smiled. "You're getting there, William. We should drink to that. What would you like? The Americans left enough liquor here to last out the century."

I settled for a scotch.

We clinked glasses and the evening took off. There was rum in Kim's drink. By now I could smell it on her breath. I wondered if she had a bug in her shoulder bag. If she had it wasn't doing much good, not with all that Armenian music in the background. The waiter took the dishes away and brought more drinks. No bill was presented then or later. Kim's ID card was better than American Express; the bill never came.

My drinks got stronger and it was a good thing I grew up on moonshine back in Beaumont. My folks were country people come to the city and one of my uncles who stayed on the farm still ran a little corn for home consumption. It was going to take more than scotch to make me say the things Kim wanted to know.

"This stuff is making me woozy," I told her after the third drink.

"You're in good hands. You will be in good hands after we get back to the hotel."

She was getting bawdy; up till now all she did was talk dirty. I wasn't coming on as fast as she expected, and this caused her some concern.

"You're not a fag, are you?" she said. "It's all right if you are, but I hope you're not."

I had enough liquor to be boastful. "Let's go back right now and you'll see how much of a fag I am. I'll show you what a man can do."

"Don't get sexist, William. When we go to bed, it will be on terms of complete equality."

It didn't turn out that way: Kim begged for it once we got started. I hoped the spooks at the other end of the bug wouldn't make a note of her sexual submission. It must be hard to listen to stuff like that without getting excited. Maybe they gave them saltpeter, the way they used to in the old Regular Army. I was afraid she would turn out to be a lousy lay, what with the booze and all those Marxist inhibitions. I need not have worried.

"Oh Jesus fucking Christ, that feels good," she yelled when I shoved it into her as far as it would go. The reference to JC must have been a holdover from the convent years. She was wet and ready and I was hard as a billy club. "That's it, William! That's it!" she sobbed, clawing at my back, and if her fingernails hadn't been sensibly socialist they would have done plenty of damage to my hide. I rode her and then she rode me. We rolled alll over the bed in a tangle of sheets until finally exhaustion forced us to stop and we lay together sweating and breathing hard, unable to go on but knowing we'd be at it again as soon as we took time to rest.

Kim's long black hair had come undone; so neat under her cap, it now hung down to her breasts. It was damp and shiny. I ran my fingers through it, but she pulled away from me and sat on the edge of the bed with an odd, embarrassed look on her face that didn't go with her performance of a few minutes before.

"What we need is another drink," she said.

"For the drink you buy it in the restaurant," I said.

"Why are you talking like that?"

"That's what they told me today when I called room service. There wasn't any."

"Never mind that. I'll call down."

We got a bottle, glasses, and ice. Kim fixed the drinks and raised her glass in salute, something Western women never do.

"Now we have shared our bodies and we are loyal friends," she said.

What can you say to stuff like that? "To friendship," I said.

"Where would you like to go?" she said, darting a look at me. The booze was wearing off, or she hadn't been as drunk as she acted.

"Right now I'd rather stay in bed."

I reached for her, but she wasn't ready for more hay-hay. She rattled the ice in her glass and tapped her foot. A little impatience she wasn't quite able to control. Maybe I was overplaying the sappy act.

"I mean tomorrow," she said. "I can make suggestions, but you must decide where you want to go. There are places you can't go for security reasons. The rest of the country is open to you. You can always see Ho Chi Minh City on your way back."

"I was thiking that. Is the border country off limits? If it isn't, I'd like to go there. Up where Vietnam, Laos and Campuchea meet. I'd better start calling Cambodia by its right name. That country up there, the magazines back home call it the Golden Triangle. Are they lying when they call it the most lawless place in South East Asia? Bandits? Dope smuggling, the lot?"

"Why do you want to go there?"

Ice got in her mouth when she drank. She chewed on it, looking away from me, waiting for my answer.

"Because I've read about it," I said. "Because I asked Major Phuong if there was anti-government guerilla activity and he denied it. I understand why he had to deny it, but I didn't believe him."

"Major Phuong has his duty to perform," Kim said.

"I said I understood his reasons. Look. You've been honest with me, something I hardly expected. Allow me to be just as honest and say I don't want a guided tour of the places your government wants me to see. I'm sure you've made great progress with new dams, roads, bridges, schools, and hospitals. I'll give an honest account of what I see, but that's not all I want to write about. I don't want people back home to think I traveled this country with blinders on. What would be the point of coming, if I did that?"

Kim finished her drink and got back into

bed with me. "There's no need for a freedom of the press speech," she murmured, pressing her body against mine. "You can go anywhere you like as long as you're with me."

I went where I wanted to go, and she liked it as much as I did.

SEVEN

THE GOLDEN Triangle is east of the city of Pleiku. I'd been to Pleiku before, while we were fighting for what passed for democracy in South Vietnam. To get to Pleiku you have to travel north through half the country, then go through the mountains, and there can be plenty of fog in there a good part of the year. When there was a war on, it was a dangerous place to be.

We started early in the morning in what looked like a Russian copy of a British Land Rover. It had big wheels, a four-wheel drive, a canvas roof to keep off the rain and sun. The Russian Rover was a roomy vehicle; the engine was no more than adequate for its size, and before we left the city Kim stopped at a government commissary to stock up on supplies. No money was involved: she signed a requisition with two carbon copies.

She said the supplies — tea, GI Spam, sugar, crackers, evaporated milk — were for when we got east of Pleiku and into the Triangle, where there were few hotels or eating places.

That part of the country was still being developed, she explained, and soon would be. I couldn't decide if she was putting me on, or had reverted to her offical self in the harsh light of the day. There was no real change in her attitude, just a quiet watchfulness, a little more reserve in what she said. I couldn't decide if she had doubts about me. There was always the chance they'd taken my prints from one of the glasses I'd been using and matched them against their file of American "war criminals." Hardly likely but not pleasant to think about. All intelligence people play their games.

I thought she'd have to get clearance to take me into the Triangle, but nothing was said about it, and I didn't ask. There was no way of knowing if she had called Major Phuong before we left. If she had it had been from the government store, not the commissary, where she made one more stop to get cigarettes. Because I had been with her the rest of the time, from bed to breakfast and then to the car pool to get the Rover. I stayed in the car for the second stop and by my watch she was in there for seven minutes, which seemed a litle too long because it was early and there were very few customers.

I offered to drive; she said there was no need, she liked to drive. It was better if she drove because she knew the road signs and I didn't.

I was glad to leave Saigon, because when you have so many bad memories of a place it's no pleasure to see it again. In the war years it was shabby and violent; now it was just shabby, with all the cracks of a failed economy showing. I'd been told about the half American, half Vietnamese children left over from the stinking war. Now I'd seen them for the first time, and I didn't like what I saw. Most of them lived in the street, begging and stealing to live. Some had become child prostitutes, though such rotten things don't officially exist in this rice-paddy socialist republic.

Kim saw me looking and said, "Poor things, we're trying to work out an arrangement with the Americans, but all we get is capitalist doubletalk. They'd use these poor kids for propaganda purposes, and we can't allow that, don't you agree?"

As an independent observer I said, "Why not ship them to the States and get rid of them?"

"That's not how these things work," she said.

We drove north on a good road with not much traffic. The Hanoi-Saigon trains were running again, Kim said proudly, and running on time, she added, but it was better to go by car. Anyway, no trains ran to the Golden Triangle. She smiled, seeming to say a car was more intimate.

The road went along the coast after an hour, and it was cooler then, with the Rover going at a good clip and the sea breeze blowing in through the open sides and making the canvas roof flap. We passed fishing villages with houses built on stilts; boats with the oddly shaped sails of that part of South East Asia were coming in with the morning catch. All along the coast there were palm trees bending in the hot wind; it might have been a color picture in a travel folder. The only things that spoiled the scene were the enormous portraits of Uncle Ho at one-mile intervals along the road.

Between the portraits of Ho were the patriotic posters I had seen too many of in Saigon. They all said the same thing: how wonderful life was now, but to keep it that way they had to work harder every day of their lives. That was how Kim translated the first one, and back in Saigon they'd been plastered on walls; here, in the country, they were tacked to trees or standing by themselves on wooden supports. I didn't mind the posters as much as I did the portraits; their effect was infinitely monotonous; it was as if the coast highway between San Francisco and Los Angeles had been desecrated with hundreds of pictures of Yasser Arafat. Except that Yasser has a nicer smile.

In some ways the road was familiar to me, and that was understandable, because I'd been over this stretch of road many times, mostly by chopper, now and then by truck. Now the only signs of the war were the ruined hulks of American tanks and heavy artillery brought there to serve as monuments to the socialist struggle for peace. These wrecked objects had stainless-steel plates attached to them, but not once did I see anyone taking the slightest interest. Maybe by now they had become too familiar, like the Civil War cannon on the courthouse lawn.

Everything was quiet now, no rumble of artillery, no rocket attacks by choppers, no mortar and machine gun fire from the VC. Back then there were places in South Vietnam where it never seemed to get quiet. Maybe there were lulls in the uproar of war, but it was hard to remember it. Or it could be that in the quiet times, the noise went on in your head.

Kim glanced at me. "You haven't said how you like it."

"It's beautiful," I answered. "It won't be easy to describe when I get back. I could have brought a camera, but I get poor pictures even with the best cameras. The ones that are supposed to do all the work."

Kim took a cigarette from the pack on the dashboard and lit it. She smoked the Major's brand; it smelled like a burning sofa.

"Perhaps it's just as well you didn't," she told me. "With a camera you don't have to think even if the pictures come out well. The memory is a richer source of art, wouldn't you say?"

You can take the girl out of Georgetown, but you can't take Georgetown out of the girl.

"Probably," I hedged, not wanting to get in over my East Texas head. "What's that over there? I mean that long line of hollows grown over with brush. It goes on for so long."

I knew what they were, but anything to reinforce my visting fireman identity.

Kim glanced at the defoliated jungle beside the road. Her eyes were bitter. "Those were made by B-52 bombing raids," she said. "It seems the Americans couldn't do enough for us. Americans want to change the world not only politically but physically. Watch out, they'll do it to Canada some day."

I thought that was kind of extreme, even for this one. It still bothered me, these outbursts of hers. Everything she spouted was right in line with Communist Party bullshit and yet there was a tinny ring to it. Not because it had been drilled into her, but because it was a mite

106

off key, as if she knew how to play all the right notes but the music still didn't come out right.

We stopped for lunch in a pleasant village, the best looking I'd seen along the coast. The houses were small and trim, most of them with one side open to the weather but protected by the deep eaves of a grass roof. The houses were set apart by hedges and low trees, so that one house was only half visible from another and difficult to see from the road. An orderly yard containing low-walled coops for chickens and a shed with stalls for cows adjoined each house. Here and there, between the fields and in the trees, stood the white-washed waist-high columns and brick walls of Vietnamese tombs.

We had beer and seafood under a grass roof, and the proprietor, a one-legged man, set a transistor radio on the table along with the food. I reached over to turn it off; Kim stopped me and said it wouldn't be polite.

"I was just going to turn it down," I said.

"That's different," she said. "I'll do it."

She didn't turn it down much. The crippled proprietor watched us. It had been nine years since the Americans had left, and I wondered how the one-legged guy got that way. From the look he gave me, it must have been our side. Tough shit! I knew a guy back in the States who'd came out of Nam missing his arms and legs and his eyes. The proprietor went away for a while.

After a second bottle of beer Kim became more spontaneous and relaxed. She told me the name of the village we were in and a little of its history. It had been razed by the Americans because it was so strongly pro-VC . I looked

107

around trying to hide the jolt she'd given me. No damn wonder it looked better than the other villages we'd been through: Luc An, as it stood now, was no more than elevn years old. Shit yes! That's where we were, in the village of Luc An, and I'd been part of the force that wiped it off the face of the earth. It wasn't as famous as Ben Suc, which got into the American newspapers and caused one of the biggest scandals of the war. That had to be wiped out too, and so had others, but Ben Suc was the one the press picked up on and cried over.

We hadn't killed more than four or five hard-core VC who tried to make a run for it. Just the same we moved in with choppers and sealed off the village before the huge bulldozers were flown in by Skycranes, the biggest helicopters in the world. Before the dozers came we rounded up the villagers and took them away to a relocation camp. I got to stay behind and I remember how the dozers just flattened the village. Nothing got in the way of those big bastards: houses, trees, brick tombs went flat before they finished. There was a heavy fog that morning and the big dozers looked like science-fiction monsters coming through it. The destruction of a village where people have lived for centuries—a thousand years, I heard it said—wasn't such a great thing to look at. But it had to be done because nothing else had worked.

" I read what the Americans did to Ben Suc," I said. "I didn't know they destroyed any more villages that way."

Her eyes glittered and it seemed her fanaticism had more depth after a few drinks. "They destroyed hundreds of villages," she said.

"But the way they obliterated Ben Suc and this village was very special. We may never know where the orders originated, perhaps in the White House itself, but we do know that several of the American generals protested against it. Don't forget, these men were as evil, as cruel as they make them, and even they didn't like it. This village, Luc An, was the most prosperous in the area, its people the most unified against American aggression. A village wanting nothing more than peace!"

Like hell!, I thought, nodding seriously at her. Luc An, so happy and smiling on the outside, harbored one of the most vicious bands of VC guerrillas in the South. More than that, its so-called peaceful fishermen were landing foreign agents from Russian submarines. They were warned to knock it off or be punished; they didn't listen. So they got zapped.

"It's a fine little place," I said.

The guy with one leg was back on duty, keeping busy but watching all the time, and I wondered if he was one of the VC we shot that morning. We killed a few, a few got away. Maybe this guy got away with a leg wound that turned gangrenous later. Kim saw him hanging around and called him over. He came smiling on his crutch, a small man in his late thirties who looked much younger. It's the smooth skin and the thick black teenybopper haircuts that do it.

I wasn't surprised when he spoke English; the Americans had been in his country for a long time, even the Southerners hated us, but it helps to know your enemy's language. He had calm black eyes and a smile like a painted doll, and even with the missing leg he looked like a dangerous man. I wondered what he did besides running a fishfood restaurant. Kim told me they were old friends. That was easy to believe.

He stood there making polite conversation. Kim prompted him to say he'd been there the morning the Americans flattened his village. I was a friendly Canadian and it was all right to talk.

"I was the village secretary," he told me in stiff English. "By that I mean I dealt with taxes and supplies. The other village secretary was the education officer. He was responsible for the schools and the propaganda meetings, the anti-American slogans. The village chief supervised our work and everything else in the vilage. Our job was to win the hearts and minds of the people. It was not hard, Mr. Stewart. The people yearned for freedom."

"Tell about how the ARVN soldiers tried to counter what you did," Kim said.

"Ah yes! Sometimes they came and tried to put on their own town meetings and festivals. Americans called them Hamlet Festivals." A little contemptuous smile here. "Not the play by William Shakespeare, of course. Hamlet, village. When they came our own village political structure was dismantled...so long as they remained. They came to educate and to intimidate at the same time. They were indecisive because the Americans, a few political officers, usually accompanied them, always hoping to win us over with the carrot and the stick. ARVN

110

intelligence set up interrogation centers and searched for draft dodgers while others, a special team of entertainers, put on a program of propaganda songs and popular love songs for the women and children. Sometimes a medical team gave injections and handed out pills. This didn't always work—hardly ever, Mr. Stewart—because the people were afraid of being poisoned by the AVRN...."

I made notes. Having to face him made me uneasy even though years had passed and I was camouflaged by a beard, contact lenses and horn-rimed glasses. There wasn't any way he could have remembered me. I hadn't stalked around his frigging village hoisting babies on a bayonet. No matter: this guy was a presence from the past.

"Don't you have any questions?" Kim said. The Vietnamese waited.

Pencil poised, I said, "Comrade Diem described how you rebuilt this village. Do you think it will ever be the same?"

"It is the same, Mr. Stewart. It would be different if the Americans had destroyed buildings that had existed since the beginning. They didn't. Our homes are flimsy things and have been replaced hundreds of times. The great American cities will not be rebuilt so easily."

His calm eyes got hot when he said that. Don't ever be fooled by that so-called Oriental calm; it has more to do with their expressionless faces than anything else. I've seen them go wild shrieking crazy over nothing at all.

"Then you think they will be devastated?" I said.

111

"Yes," he answered.

I was about to say something along the lines of "Well, it was nice talking to you" when he bowed and left us. I didn't see him after that. Maybe he went to plan the nuking of Los Angeles.

We drove on through the baking afternoon. We left Da Lat behind us and stayed overnight at the next big city, Nha Trang. I'd been there. There wasn't much to see, and we were tired. Kim was quiet and ready for sleep after we'd rolled around for an hour. I lay awake for a while looking at her young face relaxed in sleep, her long black hair floating on the white pillow. Her bag was on the table on her side of the bed. It was a small hotel in a small city and everything was quiet except for a few army trucks going by.

I lay watching her and thinking she might be a way to get Albergo out. The authority she was armed with made that seem possible. All the way north, no one questioned it, had asked to see her "papers." Everywhere there was deference to her official position, and it wasn't because we hadn't seen plenty of police and soliders. We'd seeen as many as you see in any Communist country—a lot. It was like traveling through Germany with a high-ranking Gestapo official during World War Two. There had been a few moments when it looked as if some uniformed policeman might stop us, especially in the cities, but it hadn't happened. They looked and saluted and that was all.

Of course it was the uniform and the official vehicle that made it all so easy. That and the

112

fact that Vietnam was a country closed to most foreigners made it so easy for foreigners to travel because they always had an official guide. In the cities I did see a few white foreigners, but none without someone in a uniform like Kim's. As in Russia they were invariably women, all young, all determined-looking, all carrying the shoulder bag with the automatic pistol in it. Maybe the pistol was for the foreign guest's protection, but it was also to use on the guest if he turned out wrong and tried to run away.

A few guides I'd seen had been watching over two foreigners. Never more than two; that must have been what they considered a safe limit. Albergo could be my second man. Kim was the resolute type, and there were problems there that hadn't been faced yet. I would have to think hard before I did anything.

A truck backfired and her hand came from under the pillow holding the the pistol. I hadn't seen her put it there. It must have been done while I was in the john. The gun came out fast and her fingers was curled around the trigger, her eyes alert to danger. There was no fumbling with the safety catch; her thumb had pushed it off as the gun came out. That's how to do it. And I knew suddenly that what had happened to her on the hotel steps had been one of those fumbles under fire that can happen to anyone. If the dead tourist hadn't fallen on her, she would have been pumping bullets at the killer Chinaman as fast as I did an instant later. She was, I thought, no slouch with a gun, not that I really doubted that she was; it was good to have it confirmed in such a safe way.

113

She smiled when she saw there was nothing to shoot at. "Did it wake you too, William?" she asked, putting the pistol out of sight. "You see how well protected you are? Actually there's nothing to be protected against. Can't you sleep?"

The trucks were gone and there were no sounds at all. "I was dozing," I said. Maybe she hadn't been asleep after all.

"We'll go to sleep now," she said, turning over on her side.

She was nervous or she wouldn't have reacted to a backfire. They don't sound the same as gunshots. I settled down beside her, thinking it wouldn't be so hard to take the pistol away from her. But what happened after that? I would have to be ready to use it without a moment's hestitation. We could come to no agreement; threats would be useless as bribes. She would give her word and break it, as I would. All her efforts would be directed toward killing me or bringing me to socialist justice. It would be a long ride home.

Another day's drive took us over the mountains to Pleiku. It rained several times and the wet mountains were incredibly green. It was so peaceful that it was hard to believe how much fighting had gone on there in the last stages of war. There were more soldiers on the road than there had been; no one stopped us. Going down into Pleiku I could see the line of mountains on the far side of the city, and Kim didn't have to tell me the Golden Triangle was over there.

'What do you expect to find, William?' Kim said.

114

"I don't know," I said. "I'd just like to see it. You know how it is when a place you haven't seen captures your imagination? I suppose it's the name. I once knew an Englishman who was fascinated by the names of places in the American Southwest. Places they used to set western movies in: Tombstone, Lordsburg, I forget the other names, But he was fascinated by them and always wanted to see them."

We were coming into Pleiku, sprawling and industrial. "Did he get his wish?" Kim asked.

"I don't know," I answered.

"I hope you won't be disappointed."

"I doubt it. I'm not hard to please."

"That's good to hear," Kim said, smiling. "It sounds sensible and down to earth. I just happen to know it isn't true. You're like me. You want things you don't talk about."

I said, "Maybe we should get together and see what they are."

Kim stopped the Rover in front of the Pleiku hotel where we were to stay for the night, a 1930's modern building with four floors. It didn't look busy.

"We'll see," Kim said. "But first there must be complete honesty, right?"

"Right," I agreed.

We went in.

EIGHT

THE ROAD wound up toward the pass, and that early in the morning there were patches of fog that wouldn't burn off till later when the sun came up strong. To get out of the city we had to drive along a wide avenue once lined with French-style mansions. A few were left, but mostly it was factories of one kind or another. Workers wearing smog masks, most of them on bicycles, were streaming into the factories when we drove past at ten minutes to five.

It was Kim's idea to get an early start. Now, an hour later, we were following the twists of the road as it unrolled in front of us. Kim was bright and almost gay for so early in the morning. And she was nervous.

She sang a little song in Vietnamese. It sounded like a children's song; she told me it was the new "worker's" song. After that it didn't sound so gay.

"Wake up and greet the new day," she chided me. "Arise, spring from your bed, your work awaits you. That's part of the song."

The road climbed, doubled back, then

116

climbed again. I looked at the mountains. This was wild country, guerrilla country; the mountains were so jagged, the gorges so narrow, that even choppers weren't much use. We had learned that during the war when we found it almost impossible to penetrate part of the Triangle. There were no foothills; the mountains just rose up to become peaks with clouds drifting across the highest places, and because of the fog, it was a bad place for aircraft of any kind. It was hard to believe that these mountains could be crossed if you didn't follow the road, yet it had been done by the VC guerillas during the war and was still being done by the drug bandits who lived there now.

We drank coffee from thermos bottles while Kim drove. The hotel breakfast hadn't been much; they weren't trying too hard to please foreigners. I looked at the jumble of mountains and wondered how I was going to find Albergo. He had given his father the name of the village, Cheo Reo, his camp was near, and because it was a village it had to be on the road, or close to it, but there had to be a reason for stopping there that wouldn't make Kim suspicious. By now I had decided that grabbing her and the car was the best way out. But first I had to find Albergo; the man had been long in this country and maybe he had some ideas of his own. Until I found the son of Little Caesar, Kim and I would continue as loving friends.

How did I feel about her? That was a hard question to answer and time hasn't made it any easier. I suppose I liked her in spite of what she was, all the rubbish she spouted. No matter what they say, other people don't make us what

117

we are; we are our own creations. Kim had give up the soft life to come back to this. Like the rich radical who makes bombs in the basement of her daddy's townhouse, Kim believed in what she was doing, or thought she did, and it comes to the same thing in the end. Not all the rich radicals go back to the charge-card life when they're thirty, for some it's too late by then. They put themselves in a postion where they're stuck with what they have.

But I felt no qualms about using her to get Albergo out. It hadn't come to that, but it might, and if and when it did, she would just have to accept it as part of the dangerous life she had chosen to live. It might get her shot, or sent to the mines, but that, too, was part of the game.

"Isn't it beautiful, William?" she said, indicating the fog shrouded mountains.

The mountains looked like an illustration from *National Geographic*, all misty and mysterious, and with the sun breaking through, they were beautiful. She had to change gears a lot as the road dipped and climbed.

"I never saw anything like it," I said.

"That's why I wanted you to get out early. After a while you'll see a river far below. The road follows the river gorge and you'll be glad I'm such a good driver when you see it."

We saw the river; it twisted like the road. The road was clear of fog except in the hollows and the air, though still wet, was getting warm. Once we started into the mountains we saw no one at all, not a soldier, not a peasant, and certainly no bandits. The top of the world was quiet.

Then the road was straight, or straighter than it had been, and we were coming down out of the mountains that cut the Triangle off from the rest of the country. It got hotter as the road wound down and we saw people and houses for the first time. There were peasants on the road and they looked after us as we passed.

"I'm hungry," I said when we'd been on the road for four hours. We had come to no villages yet. "Isn't there anywhere we can stop to eat?"

"We'll come to the first village in about an hour," Kim said. "But if you're very hungry, we can stop now. You saw the supplies I got in Ho Chi Minh. You want to eat *that?*"

I said I wanted to eat something and Kim laughed and pulled off the road, no longer so narrow. We ate GI Spam on crackers and drank tea she made on a canned heat stove. After we got through Kim smoked while I made notes in my book.

I looked up and said, "Where are we? I mean, what's the name of the province, the district? So far I've written; 'On Wednesday we had a picnic lunch on the side of a mountain.'"

Kim named the province and the district. "The village we'll be coming to is called Cheo Reo," she said. "Then we'll cross a river and the we'll be in another administrative district. It's called..."

I wrote down what she told me. I hadn't expected to hit Cheo Reo on the first probe. Kim smoked and watched me write. Then she put the stuff back in the car and we were ready to take off by the time I finished my phony notes.

Kim started the car. "Anyway," she said,

"How long has it been since you've been on a picnic?"

"Years," I answered. "I can't remember the last time. That's how long it's been."

"Well it was fun, wasn't it? You know, I've guided a lot of foreign visitors, but I've enjoyed this tour more than the others." A little girlish laughter. "Of course I didn't guide them the way I've been guiding you. Naturally I don't want you to write about that part of the trip. I'm joking. But it hasn't been what you expected, has it?"

"Not a bit."

Kim put the car into gear. "Somehow or other we've become more than friends. Oh we're the best of friends, of course, but you know what I mean. Friendship and trust is the best basis for any relationship, and everything follows from that point on. Don't look so startled, William. I'm not throwing myself at your head, as they used to say in old plays I haven't seen. Ridiculous expression, that."

I looked out at the mountains. "It's been very nice," I said, the Canadian shitkicker at a loss for words. She was asking me to trust her. We were pals together and there was always the suggestion that I could tell her anything and it wouldn't get me into trouble because, although she was a dedicated Communist, a woman's heart beat beneath the uniform and she would understand.

"I haven't had many friends," she told me. The sun was hot on the canvas roof. She gave me a quick look to see how I was taking the honesty bit. "I haven't had many friends because I didn't think I needed them. Don't get me wrong when I say that, because I'm a very self-sufficient person and my work means alot to me, but you know it's nice to find someone you can be close to. When I heard I was scheduled to guide some Canadian newspaperman, I thought, Oh God, how many boring questions will I have to answer for this guy? Answering questions is part of my job, and I love my job, but you haven't seen some of the newspapermen I've had to deal with. Either they're serious as owls, with no sense of humor at all, or else they drink from flasks when there isn't a bar around, or they want to be taken to whorehouses. One guy drunker than the rest tried to put the make on me. I had him expelled from the country for that."

"Poor guy," I said.

Kim laughed. "Be honest now. Did you want to put the make on me when you saw me?"

"Sure I did, but I was afraid I'd be expelled from the country. I won't be expelled, will I?"

"Not unless I report you to the proper autrhorities. But nobody has to know about it, right?"

I thought of the bugged hotel room, the spools of the tape recorder turning while we rolled around in the sack. By now our night of love had been labeled and put away for further use. Such is romance in the world of electronics.

"Right," I said. "It wouldn't get you in trouble, what we did? Are doing?"

"No, not really," she said, giving me a quick look. "Not unless you turn out to be a spy. Unless you're that, there's no problem at all. We can be friends with the Russians without

121

being as grim about sex as they are. We like their technology, but not their prudishness. Anyway, I don't think they're as prudish as they're made out to be. Whatever they are, they're better than the Americans, who want to screw everything that moves and to hell with how much damage they do. No, I think my superiors would take a very lenient view of what's been happening between us, if they knew about it."

"Well I'm not a spy and I'm not going to kiss and tell. Your secret is safe with me, Comrade Diem."

Such lines come hard to me, but I was supposed to be a bit of a jerk.

Kim patted my knee. We were coming into a village. It had to be Cheo Reo. "I'd never get you into trouble, William," Kim said. "I'd have to struggle with my official conscience if I found you were doing something wrong, but there's no way I'd get you into trouble. Hey! Don't put that in your notebook or I'll murder you. That was for your ears only."

It was my turn to do some knee patting. "There's not much I wouldn't do for you," I told her.

Kim gripped the steering wheel, but didn't look at me. "I think I love you, William," she said. "You don't have to say anything."

Nothing more was said; there was village traffic to get through, and there was plenty of it. A water buffalo with a boy on his back got in our way. The boy grinned at us while we waited. The buffalo bellowed at the car. It was a big village and the entire population seemed to be in the street. The mountains rose up on

122

all sides of it, and it was hot, but not nearly as hot as it would have been on the flatlands. We moved on when the buffalo did. There were no foreign influences here, none of the closed-up gas stations or frozen custard stands I'd seen in the towns on the other side of the mountains. Nobody rode a honda with a transistor radio to his ear. There were no pictures of Uncle Ho.

"Progress takes time," Kim said when I mentioned it. "These people have been cut off from the world for centuries. The French failed to change them, so did the Americans, when they managed to get here. That road we came over wasn't always a road. Once it was a track. We blew it up many times during the war. There are no pictures of Uncle Ho because they keep taking them down. I wouldn't have admitted that to you four days ago. The Government makes allowances for their remoteness, their isolation. It is one of geography, not of politics. You will see pictures of Uncle Ho appearing now that I am here."

Right on cue, a picture of Uncle Ho was hoisted in front of a tea shop and secured by guy ropes. A man came forward bowing, a fat elderly Vietnamese with a skullcap. There was a lot of Chinese in him. War or no war, the Chinese or part-Chinese were a power in the country, even here in the back of beyond.

Kim spoke sharply to the part-Chinaman and he replied with many bows and silbilant sounds. Then he turned and bowed to Uncle Ho's picture. "He's explaining that they took it down to be cleared of bird droppings," Kim said to me. "That fat liar! But what can we do but be patient? Now he's inviting us in for tea. Why not? He's afraid I'll report him."

I don't think the part-Chinaman was afraid of being reported; he just wanted to get on the good side of the pretty lady in the government uniform. Guys with connections tend to get over-confident and maybe he thought there was nothing she could do to make trouble for him. He was far from the seat of government and this was the Golden Triangle. West of the Pecos, I thought, and the only law is the long-range graft paid to the right people hundreds of miles away. I didn't see any bandits, but maybe they were all disguised as buffalo boys.

It was good to get out of the sun. The part-Chinaman bowed us to a table. No transistor radio was provided to make music. The tea shop smelled of hot tea and spices. No sweat smells such as you find in other parts of South East Asia. The Vietnamese are the cleanest people in the world and bathe three times a day.

We got tea and curried chicken and sweet cakes. They had electric power, homemade in Cheo Reo, and an electric fan blew away the flies. People came to the open front of the tea shop to stare at us. They kept on staring long after they knew what we looked like, an it seemed they didn't get many strangers in this neck of the woods.

Kim waved her hand. "This is the Golden Triangle," she told me, smiling. "It isn't golden and strictly speaking it isn't a triangle. How do you like it? Disappointed it's so peaceful? "

"I told you I was easily pleased. I don't work for a tabloid. Being peaceful is okay with me."

We had finished eating. "You want to go on?" Kim asked, still smiling. "We can if you like."

I looked out at the teeming street. "Let's

stay on for a while. I'd like to walk around and look at the town. What goes on here anyway?"

"What you see. People come down from the mountain valleys to trade. They buy and sell things. Economic controls haven't been imposed here yet. The Government has a flexible policy and they take it one step at a time. Our socialist revolution isn't a rigid thing: we're open to experiment. You want to do the town now?"

"Sure. Let's see what's going on in Cheo Reo."

There was a lot going on, all of it having to do with the life of the village. Other pictures of Uncle Ho were in place; all were the same. In fact, they're the same all over Vietnam. It's that famous picture you used to see on tee shirts back when the longhairs were protesting the war, marching on Washington, getting gassed by the cops. It's out of favor in the States, but in Vietnam it's still the Number One poster.

A crowd of kids followed us. I'll say one thing for the Golden Triangle: the kids there were livelier and better fed. So were the grownups; Kim's uniform interested them, but they weren't in awe of it. I looked for men without the peasant stamp on them. I knew I would have spotted them if they'd been there. Lawless men have a different look even when they're trying to pass as one of the boys. The guys I saw were all unmistakably peasants or shopkeepers; there wasn't a drug smuggler or bandit in the lot.

There wasn't much to see in Cheo Reo, one long street clinging to the side of a mountain, and from the street I could see the paths that climbed up into the mountains; people were

125

coming down with baskets on their heads, hurrying to do business in a place that was all business. Passing one house I caught the whiff of opium, but that was no evidence of criminal activity; opium smoking is as old as Vietnam itself. It wouldn't be easy to hang around much longer without a good excuse. Right then there was none that I could think of.

Kim came up with one: she said she'd like more tea. "Then we'll go on, I promise you," she said. "You're not bored, are you, William? After all, the Golden Triangle was your idea."

I doubt if many government guides talked to their charges in that way. But then we did have a special relationship.

"I'm not a bit bored," I said. "I'd like to stay here and get the feel of the place. What's the good of rushing through one village after another like a tourist? Write about daily life in a mountain village, that's what I'll do. Everything that happens in the course of a day."

Kim didn't seem to care. "Sure, if you like. You see what happens here. Nothing happens here."

But she was wrong. Five men walked in and proved it. Five men: two white, two yellow, one black. All were somewhere in their thirties. I knew the black was the boss man even before he pointed and one of the whites jerked a cord and dropped the bamboo curtain that faced the street. It fell with a crash, raising dust. The other white man turned on the lights, yellow and flickering in paper shades. Kim didn't move, neither did I.

The black, big and barrel-chested, looked at

Kim's bag lying on a chair she'd pulled close.

"Don't even think about it," he said with no particular menace.

The two yellow men were Chinese; one of them took the bag and slung it over his shoulder. Both Chinese were small and slim, quick in their movements. The two whites weren't much more than thirty and had the dissipated look of All-American boys gone wrong. They carried Colt forty-fives in leather holsters fastened to their belts. The two Chinamen had USAF .38 revolvers in shoulder rigs. Only the black carried a long gun, a Savage Model 77E slide-action combat shotgun. The Marines used it in the war, when there was close work to be done. A five-shot, 12-gauge, one hell of a weapon. It's a heavy, solid weapon; in the black's hand it look small.

"You took long enough to get here, Rainey," he said. The owner of the tea shop stuck his head in from the door of the kitchen. "Scat!" the big black said. "Let's see your passport, Rainey. I wouldn't like it if there was a switch along the way."

I gave him the passport and he flipped it open with one hand. Kim turned to look at me, then stared straight ahead. The black thumbed the pages and put the passport in his pocket. He wore a cowboy hat on the back of his shaved head; a leather thong cinched it under his chin. Marine Corps was stamped all over him. He was sure to have been a very mean sergeant, and I don't think he ran away from the war because he'd been afraid.

"I guess you're Rainey," he said. "You'd better be. It won't be hard to find out for sure."

127

"Where's Albergo?"

"Not here. Let's go."

One of the Americans was drunk or stoned. He said, "Over the fields and through the woods to the godfather's house we go." He grinned idiotically; no one else cracked a smile. His blond hair, going grey, had been hacked off in a sort of crew cut. It stood up all over his head, giving him the look of an aging punk rocker. His pale blue eyes were watery and tired.

"Move it!" the black said. He carried the short-barreled shotgun with his finger resting on the trigger guard. The shotgun had seen hard use, but was well cared for. I wondered why the others were armed with handguns instead of something bigger. Maybe he didn't trust them with something bigger.

The curtain was rolled up and we went out with the tea shop owner tagging along. He wsasn't scared of these guys, just wary of them, unwilling to get more involved than he had to. The wisdom of the East: smile and say as little as possible. Kids were climbing all over the Rover. The tea shop guy chased them away.

Albergo's men had come in two jeeps, old, battered, crusted with mud. "Get in, you drive, just follow along," the black said to me. He got in the back of the Rover and sat with the combat shotgun across his knees. His manner was easy and relaxed. I started the car and waited for the jeeps to move out.

The two Chinamen went first. It took a while for the second jeep to get going. The drunk or stoned white guy wanted to drive and there was an argument before he moved over to the passenger's seat. I wondered why the big black

128

didn't yell at him.

Only the kids ran after us; the grownups just looked. The tea shop owner gave a jerky little wave. Two men were taking down a picture of Uncle Ho that had been put up less than an hour before. I followed the two jeeps out past the end of town. This was where I started earning my money.

Behind me the seat creaked as the black made himself more comfortable. Kim did nothing but stare ahead. She had shown no real surprise, which made me think she'd been expecting it all along. Or it could be her training. I thought of the Chinaman I'd killed. I thought of Major Phuong. I thought of the old mobster, Albergo's father, back in New York. The pieces, if they were pieces, refused to fit.

I tried a question. "How is Albergo?"

"Don't be asking take-charge questions," the black said. "You ain't in charge of nothing yet. Maybe never will be."

"I just asked how he was."

"Sure you did. Okay, you can ask. You want to know real bad, Joe is fine. No more questions about Joe. You talk to him about him. How you like being back?"

"I see a lot of changes."

"Yeah, sure. Me, I never left. It suits me all right. Not many things I miss about the States. A few things. How is it back there?"

"A lot of people out of work. We won a war with Grenada. That's an island the size of Dallas Airport. Everybody is wearing jeans."

"Yeah, we hear that on the radio. Martin Luther King , they made a holiday out of his

129

birthday, that right?"

"That's right."

I didn't know his name. Maybe he'd tell me when he felt like it. Kim still hadn't said a word. The road climbed after we left the village. Up ahead the jeeps were traveling in low gear.

"You're following too close," the black said. "We don't want to bunch up, do we? Remember your military training, man."

I slowed down. "You expecting to be ambushed?"

"More questions. Let's keep the conversation general. You were saying about Martin Luther King. I was. They may have made a legal holiday out of him, but people won't want to observe it, you'll see. All it means is department stores will have one more sale day in the year. Don't think I'm bitter, though. I don't live there, I live here. No mind to me what they do on Martin's birthday."

A few miles after that the jeeps slowed even more and turned left onto a trail that went straight up, then leveled off and went around the side of the mountain. We had to ford a shallow river floored with rocks and gravel, and the Rover took some punishment. Up out of the river, I said, "We don't want to get this vehicle too banged up. It's got official markings. Nobody stopped it or us of the way here. It could mean safe passage for Albergo, some of the way."

"Drive right and it won't get damaged," the black said. "Not this one trip, it won't. I told you not to be talking this and that about Joe. You can tell him anything you like. He's the general, this outfit. Generals are deep thinkers.

130

Being such they don't confide their battle plan till the time is right. Hey man, does the gook lady have the power of speech or did she guide you by deaf and dumb?"

"I don't want to talk to you," Kim said.

The black snuffled; it was a kind of laugh. "Didn't ask you to talk to me. Was asking if you could talk—what the hell is going on?"

Fifty yards in front of us the wigged-out white guy had fallen out of the jeep. The jeep had stopped and the driver was yelling at him to get back in. He wasn't injured. He was pulling at his bushy crew cut and yelling back. The jeep began to back up.

The black tapped me on the shoulder. "Drive on up there," he ordered. "I been telling and telling that man. Now he's had it."

I stopped the Rover and the black climbed out with the shotgun. The two whites, arguing like hell, didn't seem to see him. "Get in the fucking jeep, Bobby," the driver was saying, shoving at the other guy. The other guy began to cry; tears ran down his face, snot leaked from his nose. A junkie in need of a fix. It was obvious now. An attack of the horrors can come on fast. "I'm sick," he whined. "I'm shaking all over. You got something stashed in the jeep. Ah Jesus! You got something, I want it." His voice rose to a scream. "You give it—I'll fucking kill you!"

"Stand aside," the black said, pushing the driver away with his free hand. "Don't mix in. You know he has it coming."

"Please, Sarge, I can handle him." The driver's eyes jumped from the black to the slobbering junkie. "You don't have to—it

131

doesn't have to be. . ."

The black's free hand came up to steady the shotgun. It boomed and the junkie went down, his head shattered, the body twitching. He wasn't jerked off his feet the way they are in the movies. That doesn't happen even with a shotgun. Inertia is the reason. The junkie just folded and fell.

The black made no move to cover the other man. There was quiet arrogance there; he was sure the other man wouldn't do anything about it. The first jeep had stopped, but the two Chinamen stayed where they were. Flies and insects were already investigating the blood-soaked corpse.

"Bury him or leave him, he was your friend," the black said. "You're better off without him."

The black called Sarge climbed in and told me to drive on. Shotshells rattled in his coat pockets when he sat down. The dead man's friend was taking an entrenching tool from the jeep. The two Chinamen were going ahead.

"You always have trouble with faggots," Sarge said. "Only here one of the faggots was a junkie, which made it worse. I'll handle it, he said. I'll look after him till he gets off the shit. Where have I heard that before? Can be done, can't be done, depends on the man is the way it is."

None of this required an answer. I looked at Kim. Her blank expression told me nothing. But she knew the fix she was in; Major Phuong and his men were a long way away. Or were they? It was even possible that she was playing some game of her own, something that had nothing to do with the political police. I'd given that plenty of thought on the way north. Now I gave it some more, and came to the same conclusion. Which was that I'd just have to wait and see which way she jumped.

The trail got narrower. Floods had washed it away in places; there were dirt slides to get over. Red light glowed behind distant mountains as the sun went down, and the engine whined in stretches where the trail was very bad. I switched on the lights and Sarge tapped me on the shoulder.

"Don't do nothing I don't tell you to do," he said.

"You want the lights off? The Chinese have their lights on."

"Never mind what they do. I tell you nothing, then you do nothing. You got to keep that in your head at all times."

"Right," I said.

"You don't have to say anything," Sarge said. "It's done by doing, not by saying. Actions speak louder than words, you dig?"

This time I nodded.

It went on like that, hour after hour. Sarge would make some comment, then lapse into silence. Curiously, for such a dangerous man, he was no kind of bully. You might even say his manner was mild, as if he saw anger as a weapon and reserved it for special occasions. I knew I'd hate to be on the receiving end when he decided to turn it loose. I don't know how intelligent he was; there are all sorts of intelligence. This guy knew his job, and maybe that was all he needed to know. He had killed the junkie-faggot without rancor: the guy was a danger to the outfit and had to be eliminated.

The Corps had trained him well. You killed when you had to. You didn't have to get too mad about it.

"Not far now," Sarge said.

Here the trail had a flat cliff on one side, a sheer, quarter-mile drop on the other. Sarge told me to crawl. He didn't have to tell me. I don't know how they got around there in the rainy season. I guess they walked, hugging the cliff wall while the rain came down in sheets.

"Down there," Sarge said after the cliff sloped back and the trail got wider. "Take 'er down nice and easy."

NINE

ALBERGO CITY was stirring by the time we got down. The two Chinamen were out of the jeep and making a lot of noise. Lights came on in the huts still blacked out; there was the blare of rock music on a radio. Amplified as by a concert bowl, the sound echoed up between the cliff walls. Then the DJ cut in with the usual, mindless DJ babble, and the Australian-accented voice seemed even weirder than the music, in that dark place, at that cheerless time of the morning.

"That's Jumpin' Jack Jackson, in Sydney," Sarge said. "We got a G.E. World Monitor short wave. Quality stuff, can pull in any station no matter where. Drive over there, that big house. We don't call them huts. Sounds primitive."

I counted twenty men before I had to pay attention to my driving. Others were probably still asleep. The ones I saw were dressed every which way; some wore combinations of GI and native clothes; there were baseball caps, Asian sombreros, and conical native hats made of grass. The majority were white, in their thirties

135

or forties. I was surprised to see one old guy, with a clipped white beard, who must have been on the bad side of sixty. The rest were Asians.

Albergo came out on the porch of his house, walking stiffly without the help of a crutch. Nobody had to tell me who he was. I had his face in my head. He didn't look like the photograph his father had shown me. In the photograph, his face was spoiled and slightly fat, the face of a spoiled adolescent with a rich father. It wasn't the kind of face you'd expect to see under a Marine Corps cap. But he had enlisted, he hadn't waited to be drafted. More than likely, it had been done to get back at the old man, who couldn't haved liked it, though the wise guys are as anti-Communist as Midwest farmers. I might hear the story from Joe Junior, not that it mattered much.

The Albergo I was looking at was thinner and older. His thick black hair had long grey streaks in it. He wore clean GI pants and shirt, a woven sombrero, and if it hadn't been for the long nose, he would have been handsome. Maybe he was handsome to women of a certain kind who are attracted to men with intense black eyes, and the rest of it isn't important.

He stood there and watched us getting out of the Rover. No anticipation showed in his eyes, no excitement, not even much interest. Kim was smoothing down her uniform, making a big thing out of it. Sarge, even with the killing, had failed to scare her after she knew she wasn't going to be shot out of hand. I think Albergo scared her. That would figure: he was a scary-looking man.

"What happened to the lovers?" Albergo said, at last. His voice was strained and hoarse, not so very different from his father's. A little of his prep school accent was left. They call it "Eastern Lockjaw," I'm told. They teach them, or they teach themselves, to drawl without moving their jaw much.

Sarge shrugged. "Had to do what we talked about," he said. "It was then or later. Guy staged a real junkie scene. Buck stayed behind to bury him. Would have done Buck too, but you said no."

Albergo rested his hand on the porch rail, taking the weight off his artificial leg. "No need to do Buck," he said. "They were getting a divorce."

Sarge laughed. Albergo didn't. "This guy okay?" he said, meaning me.

"A quick check says he is," Sarge answered. "His passport. Not for me to decide what he is."

Albergo nodded. "You come in," he said to me. "Give the woman breakfast. I have to think about her. No gang rape, Sarge, and you keep your pecker in your pants. Maybe later, not now. They get excited having her here, they can do what they always do."

Kim gave me a quick look, then went with Sarge. Albergo had these guys under good discipline. Nobody made a move. Albergo turned to go into the house, and I followed him.

The house had two rooms. It had a wood floor, cane tables and chairs, a radio transmitter on an ammunition box, a rough bookcase with a few mildewed books in it, weapons in waterproof cases. When Albergo turned I saw the Colt forty-five in his back pocket. He walked stiffly ahead of me, quick enough for a man with a metal leg. There was a tightly laced shoe on the metal foot.

Albergo eased himself into a chair padded with army blankets. His thin face was rigid, as if suppressing pain. Pain, and other things, had made him very hard, and I knew that men with all their limbs were his enemies. They weren't members of the amputee club, the pain fraternity. Compassion was as foreign to this man as disco dancing would be to a Presbyterian elder.

"Pull a chair up close," Albergo said. He switched on a short-wave radio. Some guy was ranting in Vietnamese. It was hard to hear what Albergo was saying. "I don't trust anybody," he said. "I may not be able to trust you. That remains to be seen."

I nodded.

Albergo looked at my passport, held the pages up to the light. "If it's a fake, it's a good one," he said. "Sometimes a passport can be real and the man using it a phony."

"I'm Jim Rainey, just like I say."

"I know you're Jim Rainey. That's not what I meant."

"How can you be sure I'm Rainey?"

I could tell Albergo's leg had been amputated below the knee. The shape of the metal leg showed through the cloth of his pants. He wasn't as handicapped as he might have been.

"I'm sure," he said. "My old man wouldn't let all that money just walk away. He thinks you're a good man, but wanted to be sure you didn't yield to temptation. Not being connected, not knowing what that means, a tough guy like

138

you might think he could get away with it."

"I know what it means, crossing your father's kind of people."

"Good. Then you started with the right spirit."

"Your father had me followed?"

"Eventually, after he got a line on you. Not easy, he said, the careful way you work. Hard as hell, in fact. You just disappeared for a while. Well, my old man isn't so dumb, anyway not dumb about business, so he sat down and thought it out with a little help from the cops. I mean, he kicked it around, what you'd be likely to do. A phony passport wouldn't be enough, not here in this country. Background, he figured you'd have to have some background to work your scam on the gooks. You're known to the NYPD. One of the names in your file is a scam artist named Jaffe. Meyer Jaffe. You worked with him a few times, why not this time? The old man's people looked for Jaffe, were told he'd gone to Toronto. Didn't tell anybody but the dog hospital where he boarded his pet poodle. The rest was easy. They caught up with him the day you flew out."

"They must have leaned on him hard, to get him to talk."

"I guess. You see why I don't trust anybody?"

"Meyer is an old guy, not a tough guy. I didn't expect him to die for me."

Albergo said, "I have to admire the way you worked it, the pains you took. My old man appreciated that."

"You're in pretty close contact, you and your old man."

"We have ways. A lot of things you can't

139

know about. I may tell you, if I feel like it. Some things I'll always leave out. I think I will. It depends. I'm in a precarious situation here. I have to be careful."

Albergo was off his rocker; I was sure of it. Not crazy as in straitjacket, but weird, suspicious, eccentric, *strange*! There must have been some of that to begin with; here in this paranoid society of killers, in these foggy mountains, it had taken full flower. And because he was cracked, he was all the more dangerous.

"But you're the boss here," I said.

"Uneasy is the head that wears the crown," Albergo said. "I'm the boss here because I run things in a way that makes it good for everybody. They wouldn't know how to do it themselves. A few thought they did, a long way back. I had to get rid of them. Their ideas were counterproductive. Do they still say that, or is there a new cant word? I've had to kill a few people since then, not many, an occasional bad ass with dreams of glory. You pull out the weeds so the garden may flourish."

"You're still the boss."

Albergo nodded, frowning at the thought my words brought to the fore. I was close enough to read the titles of his disintegrating books, a ragtag collection of novels, biographies, army training manuals, and cookbooks. I pictured him reading while the rain fell, slowly turning the pages, popping pills for the pain in his leg. A bottle of Demerol stood on the table beside him. Not wanting to do it, he popped a pill now.

"I run a balancing act here," he told me. "The few queers we have, I balance them against the

140

straights. Occasionally one of the straights moves over and get on the queer side of the scales. They do that, an adjustment has to be made. I weigh the gooks against the Americans. Not all the whites are Americans. You saw that old guy with the white beard. He's a Frenchman, a French army captain left over from the old days, deserted before Dien Bien Phu, knew what they were in for and beat it out of there. Sensible. The Viets don't get along with the Chinese, more problems. My balancing act, my juggling act, is a constant thing. I make a slip, drop the balls, and I'm in serious trouble."

"You seem to do it well enough."

"I do it better than that," Albergo said. "I have them well trained, but I don't give them an inch. I'm like a good lion tamer. I keep them afraid of me. They're mangy lions. They still have teeth. I don't forget that."

Tightrope walking, juggling, lion taming! Albergo must have loved the circus, as a kid.

"But they know they have a good thing here," Albergo went on. The pill was taking effect. He was more relaxed, a little dreamy. "They know they'd be up shit creek if they didn't have me to keep things straight. I fix things, I keep our outside contacts happy, I settle disputes. Without me, they'd be fucked."

"You're a prisoner of the commonwealth, is that it?"

No smile. "Yeah, I guess you could say that," Albergo said. "They wouldn't like it if I walked out on them. That's one of the problems, how much they wouldn't like it."

"Sarge knows something about it."

141

"Yeah, something. The others know nothing."

"Then what do they think I am?"

"A contact from the States. I don't tell them what your business is, the specific reason you're here. They know who my father is, how big he is in the organization. That impresses them, having the son of a top-level Mafioso as their boss. Coming here through my father, you could be anybody. Anybody. Somebody. Somebody important. That impresses them too."

"But why tell Sarge you want to get out?"

"Sarge thinks we're friends. A good man, Sarge, the black bastard. Dependable as they come, within reason, that is. I'd trust Sarge a lot quicker than any of the others. I mean, I'd trust him if there was no other way. I'd just as soon not."

"What was your reason, then?"

Now the radio was giving out music instead of talk. Albergo turned the dial until he got more talk, this time some Asian language I didn't recognize. It might have been Radio Borneo. These days the headhunters have to make do with the shrunken heads you can buy in joke shops, but they do get to listen to the news programs.

"I told Sarge because there was no guarantee you'd get here." Albergo shifted his metal leg, looking away from me as he did it. He looked back at me, trying to read my face. Finding no reaction, he said, "You could have been nailed anytime after you got off the plane. How could I be sure the secret police wouldn't catch on? I told Sarge so I'd have some kind of plan, if you didn't show. He doesn't understand why I'd want to leave this paradise. He says he'll help me, if I really want to go."

"You gave him a reason?"

"The obvious reason, what else? I want to get back to civilization. Who wouldn't?"

"Why wait all these years? Why now?"

"Okay, there was a better reason. I said there was something wrong with my leg. Something was wrong with the bone. Needed an operation or it might kill me. Gangrene. I didn't go into details."

"Is there something wrong with it?"

Albergo looked straight at me. "That's my business. It got Sarge's sympathy, made him see I wasn't running out on him. I think it did. Sarge is big on loyalty, or would appear to be. How can I be sure? I can't be sure. I have to go on what I see. I said why didn't we go out together, get the drop on the others and just take off. I knew he'd refuse. I was counting on it."

"Why?"

"Sarge can't go back to the States, not ever," Albergo said. "Remember Benson, the turncoat they called the White Cong, back in the war? The guy that was a guard in the PW camps up north? You must have heard of him. Everybody did."

I nodded. "Yeah, he got out, the end of the war. It was in the papers. The court martial came to nothing."

"They were digging too deep and called it off," Albergo said. "The defense was digging up too much dirt, the army got nervous. Bad PR, all that talk about treason, the American public

143

wouldn't like it. We were all heroes, right?"

"You're saying Sarge was like Benson?"

"A lot worse than Benson," Albergo said. "Benson never killed any American PW's, as far as we know. Benson was just a young farm guy got captured, got hungry, got beaten, got scared. So he confessed, repented, did everything they wanted him to. They gave him a uniform, an AK-47, made him a guard. A much-hated guy, not all that bad, I think. He was out to save his skin, so what!"

"Makes no difference now."

"Not to you, not to me, to the Marine Corps it still makes a difference. Sarge was no Benson. He killed guys. There were witnesses, enough of them back in the States to get Sarge hanged or jailed for life. I think they'd go all the way with Sarge, even if the dirt started flying. Big names or no big names, I think they'd go through with the trial. Big names, yeah. Would you believe colonels? Majors? Old Regular Army guys? Sour-mash drinkers, real Americans. Some of them made public confessions, donned sackcloth and ashes, and wept for the newsreel cameras. They did. Most of it was hushed up. Wouldn't do to let it be known that Colonel Plymouth Rock had turned chicken. Would look bad if the folks back home heard about blond, blue-eyed WASP fighter pilots with two last names pissed their pants when gook intelligence got a hold of them. Guys that grew up studying maps of Bunker Hill in *American Heritage*."

"I know all that."

"You don't know about Sarge," Albergo said. "Sarge went over to the VC, but not because he was scared. Sarge scared! He went along with the VC the same as he went along with the Marine Corps bullshit. The Corps gave him a rifle and sent him over here to kill gooks. He had nothing against gooks, no more than any of us. What did he know from gooks? Then he got captured and the VC treated him pretty well because he was a nigger. The propaganda thing. Sarge decided to work his scam, pretended to be convinced by their indoctrination bullshit, said hey you guys, you got something real going for you here, kiss me, I'm black, let's get married. Funny thing, he ended up as convinced as they were. Got that old VC religion, the Vatican in Moscow, the Pope, that Russian with the bushy eyebrows. Problem was his conversion didn't last. Lost his new faith, fell away like a bad Catholic. That took a while, not too long. Too much he saw he didn't like. Like the pious guy who discovers his favorite Franciscan has a Swiss bank account. Disillusionment set in, hit him hard. But he kept on saying his political prayers, all the time waiting for a chance to walk."

Albergo paused long enough to pop another pain pill. Demerol is powerful stuff, a synthetic developed during World War II when morphine was in short supply. Take it too often and too long, you get addicted. It can make you crazy.

Albergo said, "Sarge got his chance when the USAF fuckers bombed the camp. Maybe they did it to silence the sour-mash drinkers. They bombed it good, whatever the reason. Sarge got away and took me with him. I wasn't there that long before the bombing. Sarge did favors for me because he knew who my father was. How could anybody that worked for the biggest numbers bank in Harlem not know where the money went? The reason he helped me, I might be useful at some future time. When he walked, I walked. We made our way here. This country was always a hideout for badmen of one sort or another. That old Frenchman ran things then. We organized an opposition party, he came over to us, we killed off most of the original settlers, and that was that."

I wondered how Kim was doing. The camp was quiet except for the noise Jumpin' Jack Jackson was making in Sydney. Then I heard the sound of an automobile moving in low gear. It appeared that Buck was back from burying his faggot friend.

"Sarge can't go back to the States, but I can," Albergo said. "Nothing to stop me, not a black mark on my service record. I'll bet you were like me, a good, well-motivated soldier, huh?"

"You might as well be, if you're in it."

"Good thinking. I was a real good little soldier, maybe a better soldier than you. Ever win any medals?"

"A few."

"So did I. They'd never have captured me if I hadn't been wounded. But I was. Lost the leg. Don't know how hard they tried to save it. They killed some of the wounded when there was nothing else to do with them. Our side, the same. But once they got you to a hospital, they doctored you as well as they could. It was the bomber crews they had it in for. Drop bombs you're bound to hit hospitals and schools, kill

146

kids. Same difference, you mean to or not. They gave me a nice new aluminum leg, doesn't squeak or rust, better than what Long John Silver had. Had to use a crutch at first, then they put me on a cane. The cane I can do without if I have to, me and Herbert Marshall."

Herbert Marshall was an English actor who lost a leg in the First World War. After he went to Hollywood, and became a minor star, he was hailed as the pluckiest actor in pictures. He walked through all his movies, using a cane only when he got old. I'm sure all he had in common with Joseph Albergo, Jr. was the metal leg.

"You have any plan for getting out?" I asked Albergo.

"I could have. Have you?"

There was no way to hurry him along, no way to say, Listen here, Joe, isn't it time we got down to cases? He was too dangerous for that. I didn't even know what to call him. Sarge called him Joe, but maybe that was like newspaper humorists calling Reagan Ron. It was done at a distance. Could be he hated the name Joe. I didn't want him to hate me.

I said, "Using the government car and the girl is a possibility. She has good credentials, good as they come. Nobody stopped us all the way from Saigon. We could go out the same way. Back to Saigon, then bribe our way onto a foreign boat."

"You make it sound easy."

"It didn't say it was easy. I said it was possible."

"You mean you came in here without a plan?"

"How could I have a plan? I wasn't even sure

where you were, what your situation was."

Albergo studied the shoe with the metal foot in it. "You thought you'd find a cripple? Might have to carry this cripple on your back?"

Radio Borneo, or whatever it was, went on talking. Some distance from the house, men were laughing. The radio dial was beaded with moisture. It was starting to get hot.

"The only way was to see for myself," I said.

"And having seen, what have you decided?"

"You seem to get around all right."

Albergo nodded. "Me and Herbert Marshall. Did you know your gook girlfriend was a secret police agent?"

"I figured she was."

I was ready to use Kim. I didn't want to get her killed. But I knew I'd have to be careful what I said. One mistake with this guy and I could stop worrying about burial insurance.

"You just figured? You didn't know?"

"I knew. All these guides work for the secret police."

There was no way of knowing how much he knew. His father's mobster intelligence service had traced me to Toronto. Had their Asian contacts put a tail on me when I arrived in Saigon? I thought of the dead Chinaman, but knew I was trying to pin the tail on the wrong donkey.

"That's not what I meant," Albergo said. "Some agents are more agent than others. This one has connections and not just from when her old man was important here. You don't find her guiding just any slob visitor. That's for the others to do, the Swedish sociologists, the Belgian engineers. The one you got does the special jobs. You didn't get her by accident. That's what I mean."

"You know a lot about her."

"I keep on top of things. She been working on you?"

"Yeah. She's been laying down a line, the usual stuff about socialism and how lousy America is. I'm sure my room at the Hilton was bugged. They all are, probably."

"You've been fucking her," Albergo said. "I could tell, the way she didn't want to look at you."

"I threw her a few fucks."

"Is she a good lay?"

"She's very enthusiastic," I said.

"That's what's wrong with it," Albergo said. "These women are stricter than nuns. Stricter, the kind of nuns they got these days. I would think they would be harder to bang than Mother Teresa. She suck your cock?"

"Wait a minute!"

"Hey! Hey! Don't go stiff on me. The question is business, nothing to do with me. I'm putting something together here. She copped your joint, didn't she?"

Slapping his face would get me killed. He had to be good with the forty-five or he wouldn't be boss of this outfit. Anger was a waste of effort. I'd come here of my own free will. And I'd done it for money.

"Yeah," I said. "She didn't leave anything out."

"Glad you told me," Albergo said. "A guy comes in with me, I expect the truth. Don't get a bee up your ass, it's nothing personal. Okay, this one fucks and sucks a guy she hardly knows, a foreigner, and don't tell me she has

149

hot pants, there has to be a better reason, which is she was assigned to spy on you. Now the point is, did they know you were a phony, was it just a strong suspicion, or was it something else altogether? There's heavy shit here and I'd like to know what it is."

I was pretty sure Albergo hadn't talked that way when he first came to Vietnam. It was as if he had deliberately coarsened himself, using every foul-mouth expression he could think of. Lots of other guys talk that way, but there's nothing particularly obscene about it. It's just the way they talk. Albergo was different; there was cold viciousness in every dirty word he uttered. It was the leg, the missing leg, the constant reminder that he'd never be the same again. Other men learn to live with their bitterness. Some get over it. Albergo nurtured it like a delicate, poisonous flower. When he degraded others, he degraded himself.

"You like this gook? You have a soft spot for her?" His faced was so rigid, I could almost see the nerves twanging under the skin. Keeping himself under control must have been a constant effort. It can be done—it's done all the time—but every day takes you closer to the breaking point.

I said, "She's not something you throw out of bed."

No smile. Albergo never smiled. "I wouldn't want you to get carried away. There's no future in it, not even a little bit. A brief encounter, a few fucks, a few laughs, and then goodbye."

I thought I could get him off Kim by saying, "We haven't decided much. You don't think much of my idea?"

It didn't work. Albergo said, "*We* don't decide anything. I decide everything. This isn't government by committee. About the woman, you want to do it? Sarge can do it. There's no hurry. I'd like to question her first. She'll talk. The thing with the Chinaman is a worry. Why did he do it? Who is he working for? Which one of you was he after?"

Now he was talking to himself; we all do that, hardly ever out loud. He hadn't waited for my answer about Kim. Ignoring it wouldn't help. I didn't want it to be Sarge.

"I'll take care of the woman when the time comes." Sarge would use the shotgun. I didn't want her looking into the muzzle, waiting for the buckshot to blow her apart.

"What?" Albergo had been staring at nothing.

"I said I'll kill the woman when it has to be done. Quick and clean, do it so she won't feel a thing. I have nothing against her. She did nothing to me."

It was very hot now and Albergo was sweating. He didn't look healthy. His black eyes burned as if he had a fever. The fever was in his mind.

"She never got a chance to do anything to you." He wiped his face on his shirt sleeve. "I don't care how you do it. I'll tell you when. I may give her to the men before you shoot her. A treat for them, they'll appreciate the thought."

"No!" I said.

There wasn't a thing I could do to back it up. He could do anything he liked. I said it anyway. It was a dumb move to make. But I made it. Rainey to the rescue! Rainey the shithead!

151

"You don't like the idea?"

"It stinks. You know you're better than that."

"You don't know a thing about me."

"What's the percentage, doing a lousy thing like that? These fuckers must get laid back in that village. A favor to me, don't do it. The woman is my woman as long as she lasts."

Albergo shifted his aluminum leg, pushing the metal foot with the good foot. This time he wasn't so self-conscious about it.

"What will you do if I don't grant your wish?" he asked. "What can you do?"

"Nothing. I came here to get you out. We'll be working together. I'm asking a favor."

Albergo said, "You'd have it in for me if I said no?"

This guy's mind was like a nest of snakes. "I just wouldn't like it. The woman isn't all that important. What I mean is, why not let me kill her and leave it at that?"

Albergo was losing interest. "Okay," he said, wiping his face. "It was just a thought. You don't like it, we won't do it. You've had your favor, don't press your luck by asking for more. And don't ever talk to me like that again."

Albergo looked tired. The pills were making him drowsy. His eyelids were heavy. A mosquito was feeding on his hand. He just looked at it.

"Is that all for now?"

He looked up at me. "Yes, that's all for now. One last thing. Talk to the woman, see what you can find out. There's something that isn't right. I can feel it. Talk to her before I talk to her. You could save her a lot of grief if you do it right."

I stood up. "What's the drill here? Do I get to walk around?"

"Walk around all you like," Albergo said. "I mean, what harm could you possibly do?"

TEN

THEY WATCHED me walking to the hut where Kim was. Sarge was out front, sitting on an ammunition box. There were men there I hadn't seen earlier. They'd been waiting to see how my talk with Albergo went. Americans were still in the majority. I could tell the Americans from the other whites, even when they wore outlandish clothes. Their favorite headgear seemed to be the straw sombrero. They looked like prisoners in some old colonial penal colony. Prisoners is what they were, in a way.

Buck, the dead faggot's friend, leaned against one of the jeeps with his arm around the waist of a slim Cambodian kid with long black hair and the narrow, darting eyes of a street hustler. The kid carried a Colt forty-five slung from a colorfully embroidered belt. They looked very much in love, and nobody paid any heed to the groping that was going on. To Buck, it seemed, poor dead Bobby was just a memory.

Most of the Asians were younger than the Americans, the left-overs from the war. Among

154

the Asians, mostly Vietnamese, were Chinese, Laotians, and Cambodians, to make this a truly international group. One fat Guamian stood by himself, with no compatriots to keep him company. The Guam islanders were good fighters; I never heard of any of them deserting during the war. There was a tiny independence movement on Guam, but I doubted if this fat man was part of it.

"Hold up there," Sarge said when I got to the hut. He didn't get up off the ammunition box. The M-16 was in factory condition, with the Cosmolene still on it. Sarge gave the barrel a swipe with a rag. The others watched, still as statues.

"Albergo says I have no restraints on me. It's okay for me to walk around. I'm going to talk to the woman. She all right?"

"Why wouldn't she be all right? Gave her a nice breakfast. How'd it go?"

"We talked." I went in and he didn't do anything. The men had been silent. Now they were laughing, whistling, and making sucking noises. I could picture what they'd do to Kim if they got the chance.

Kim sat on a box by a window. There wasn't much light in the hut. A plate of food, some of it eaten, was on the floor at her feet. She didn't turn until I was right behind her.

"Get away from me," she said, no expression in her face, no tone in her voice. "Rainey. Is that your name? You dirty son of a bitch, is that your name or is there another one? Are you here to kill me? Is that your initiation into this gang of murderers?"

Her voice was rising. It might have been a

studied response, one more bit of business in the character part she was playing. I thought some of her anger was real.

"Be quiet," I said. "Eat the rest of your food."

"That slop! It's probably poisoned. You eat it. I don't want it."

A little lie there. There had been a lot on the plate and she'd eaten about a third of it.

"They won't poison you," I told her. Outside, two of the Americans had been working on a jeep. The engine was roaring. It stopped and started, making plenty of noise. Kim's face quivered as she looked at me. I hunkered down beside her so she could hear what I was saying.

"I'm the only thing keeping you alive." I gripped her arm hard enough to hurt. "Listen to me, do what I tell you. If you don't talk to me, you'll have to talk to Albergo. That's his name. He runs things here. What's the real story with you?"

Our faces were close. She smelled of soap and sweat. Her cap was crooked on her head. I straightened it for her. Maybe that was all I could do for her. Sarge was cleaning an M-16, but the shotgun lay beside him, ready for use.

"You heard what I told you," she said, trying to break my hold on her arm. "I'm a government guide. I report to the political police because I have to. There's nothing else. Let go of me."

I let her go. "You better tell me. You may not get another chance. I know there's more. Albergo thinks so too. You dumb bitch, don't you know what can happen to you?"

"It'll happen anyway, what can I do about it?" Now she was playing the stoic, the brave soldier ready to face the worst thing they could throw at her. Maybe she was tough enough. Sure as hell, it wasn't enough to prepare her for this.

I grabbed her, shook her. "I just saved you from a gang rape. Albergo wanted to give you to the men."

"Is that all? Maybe I'd like it. What are you going to do? Slap me?"

"I talked him out of it."

"Saved me from a fate worse than death! My hero!"

I slapped her and she took it. Her eyes blazed with defiance. "Go to hell, Rainey."

"You better tell me something I can tell Albergo. He wants to know about the Chinaman I killed. So do I. Which one of us was the target? You know all right."

"I have nothing to say. Tell him what you like. He'll kill me anyway."

"That will be the easiest part of it. Making up a story won't work, I'm telling you. He has too much information from Saigon. He says you're no ordinary guide. You get the special jobs. I believe him."

"You're no better than he is."

I picked up on that. "Then you know who he is. How would you know? All he has here is a gang of dope smugglers and deserters. It's not a resistance movement." I shook her hard. "Answer me."

Her eyes told me nothing. "I don't have to know what he is. I can see what he is."

"You're lying."

"You're the liar, you're the sneak!"

"You'll be dead if you don't open up. Stall too

157

long, I won't be able to help you. Once he decides, that's it, you're finished."

She shrugged. "I'm finished now."

It was like talking to a recorded message. "You're not finished till you're dead. Tell me something that will keep you alive. I'll tell Albergo you're coming around but still holding something back. Maybe he'll give me time to get the rest of it. He says there's no hurry. He's holding back himself. Don't you hear what I'm saying?"

"You just want to know for yourself. Why should you care what happens to me?"

"Knock it off, we're not talking emotions here. I don't want to see you killed. You can take that any way you like. How about it?"

"How about what? I don't know what you're going on about. I told you I worked for the secret police, didn't I? You were there when I reported to Major Phuong. That was my job. I didn't try to hide it from you."

"There was no special reason you were assigned to me? Albergo thinks there was. He gave reasons. They made sense."

"Albergo can think what he likes. You were under no more suspicion than any foreigner. I wasn't assigned to you. I picked you after I read your file. Major Phuong didn't object."

"What was so interesting about my file?"

She was a fearless liar. All her lies were backed by a direct, honest look. Lying is hard except for psychopaths. Then there is inner conviction. Here, with her, there was great skill, but it fell short of perfection.

"Your face interested me," Kim said. "It was serious, sensible, even kind. You owned a

158

socialist newspaper. That interested me."

"Bullshit! Try again."

"What the hell do you want me to say? That I was assigned to you by Major Phuong? All right, I'll say it. I was assigned, but for no special reason. Your socialist background, Major Phuong thought perhaps you could be persuaded to work for us."

I thought I saw a glimmer of truth here, one pin-prick of light in her blanket of lies.

"Doing what? What would a gimpy, half-assed publisher know about anything? A loser, a nothing."

"I just said there was no special reason. It's standard procedure to sound out any foreigner who might be of use. People often know things they don't think they know. People can be trained, they can be used as couriers. Major Phuong knows more than I do."

"Sure. You don't know anything."

"I sounded you out, didn't I? You don't remember our conversations about politics? What do you think all that meant?"

"I think you were doing it for your own reasons. The room at the Hilton was bugged, you gave me the standard good time for that kind of job. You were covered by the tapes."

"I was covered by you. You weren't so hard to persuade. Not about that."

"Don't make stupid jokes. Tapes or no tapes, you were working for yourself. You had to earn your pay, but your own interests were always up front. Don't be dumber than you sound. There's not that much time."

She stared at me. Thirty seconds went by. They were still revving up the jeep. Someone was singing.

"You're hopeless," I said. "There's nothing I can do for you. I'm going out to see what's happening. I have the freedom of the camp. All you can do is sit here and wait for it."

I turned to go. Kim watched me. Then she said quickly, "I can tell you what I think," she said.

"About the Chinaman?"

"Yes." I went back to her. She said, "I don't think the Chinese was trying to kill me. What reason would he have? I'm not important. He was sent to kill you. Don't talk, ask questions, let me talk. Somehow or other, Albergo's enemies learned you were coming to bring him. They didn't want that, so they sent an assassin to prevent it. That makes sense, doesn't it? What I'm trying to say, it didn't make sense then. It does now. I had no way of connecting you with Albergo, how could I? But now that I know the connection, it has to be it. Albergo's father is a notorious American gangster and . . ."

"How do you know that?"

"I said let me talk. This Albergo's name has been in the Saigon newspapers. There's always talk about ridding this part of the country of drug smugglers and criminals. It never comes to anything because certain people in government always block it. People in Hanoi as well as Saigon. Everybody knows they take bribes, but they're too powerful to be touched. That's how I know about Albergo, this Albergo. The newspapers say he is part of the Mafia, even here."

"And they know about his father, in Saigon?"

"The newspapers say the American Government is controled by the Mafia. The Albergos, father and son, are always mentioned together."

"Get on with it, for Christ's sake."

"Shut up and don't talk. It stands to reason the father has many gangster enemies. The underworld is international, isn't it? Organized crime has branches everywhere. I think the father's enemies, his rivals, found out you were coming here, they got in touch with their associates out here and arranged for the Chinese killer to get rid of you."

What she said was possible. I just didn't believe her. But it might be something to tell Albergo if I couldn't get Kim to tell the truth.

"Why would they wait till I got here?"

Kim had an answer for everything. "They didn't find out till after you left the States."

That was possible too. Albergo's goons hadn't been able to catch up to me in Canada. I was already on my way when they shook the truth out of Meyer. Kim might be getting at the truth. Truth through lies? Well, it happens.

"Could be," I said.

"I'll bet Major Phuong has traced the dead man back to Manila or Hong Kong. It has to be that. I can't think of anything else."

I gave her a sour look. "You mean you can't think of any more lies. You've told me nothing I couldn't have figured out for myself. Forget the Chinaman, what about you?"

"I was with you. How could I have anything to do with it? I was in the same danger."

"Nobody said you had anything to do with it. You're screwing around, you silly bitch.

You're so smart you're stupid. Don't you know what's right outside that door? There's a guy with a shotgun. You saw what it did to the junkie. Boom, no head! You've got a nice face. You won't have it long, believe me. One more time is all I'm going to ask you. What the fuck are you up to?"

Kim looked away from me, really frightened for the first time. It takes a while to get through to some people, especially the smart ones. Kim belonged to the elite of this socialist paradise. Her political clout opened doors, made people get out of her way. There must have been considerable satisfaction in that. Here, in Albergo City, it was as useful as a used Kleenex.

"I have to think about it," she said, no longer defiant. "There is more involved than myself. You have to give me time—get me time—or I won't tell you anything. Be honest, is there a chance for me?"

"I don't know. You wanted an honest answer. There it is. The problem is, there's nothing I can offer Albergo. Money won't do it. He's a drug smuggler, must have more money than he needs. I can't bargain with him, no way. All I can say, I'll do the best I can for you. Now listen. If I'm going to stick my neck out, it has to be worthwhile. You still won't tell me?"

"I said I have to think about it." She sounded angry. "You may be using me, how can I tell? For all I know, you may be ten times worse than the worst man here."

I squeezed her arm. "Settle down. You're getting mad at the wrong guy."

Kim looked at me. "I didn't mean what I said.

162

I'm sorry. It wasn't so bad, the two of us together."

Was this another act? No way to tell. "It was all right," I said. "It was pretty good."

"You have a way with words, Rainey. Is that your real name?"

"The only one I've got."

Kim put her hand on mine. "I'm counting on you, Rainey. Let me think, then come back."

I nodded. "If Albergo doesn't grab me first. I'll come back, but you've got to stop lying. All you have to know about me is, Albergo's father hired me to bring his son out. I got a lot of money to do it. I'm a merc, a mercenary. I fight in wars and do dangerous things for money. It's all I know and I'm too old to change. People don't approve of what I do—too bad. This is a one-time job, I'm not one of the old man's goons. And no matter what you think, I'm no killer. That enough for you?"

"Yes, I know you're telling the truth. It's so simple, it has to be the truth. Come back, Rainey, I'm terribly afraid. No more lies. I'm scared to death."

"Stay that way," I said.

I went out and Sarge was still there on the ammunition box. "She throw you out?" he said. "I wouldn't let her do that to me."

It would be hard for anybody to throw Sarge out, with or without the Marinne shotgun. For a killer, he sounded like a simple man. I wasn't so sure.

The others were still waiting for some action. They watched me as I walked past Sarge and went down to the shallow river and scooped up water and splashed it in my face. Up so high the water was bone-chilling cold. I drank some of it. I hadn't eaten yet.

Distanced from the camp, I was able to get a better look at it. Heavy machine guns in sandbagged emplacements could stop anything coming down the steep, narrow road, and the same guns, protected by the overhang of the cliff, could be used for antiaircraft defense. This was more a gorge than a valley and attack from the air would be difficult, even for choppers. They could come in after a barrage of rockets, but they would still have to face massed fire from the heavy machine guns.

There was no sign of Albergo. The rest of them watched me as I wandered down to the end where the river came in through the gap in the rock wall. Going out that way would be a bitch: the gap was narrow and studded with jagged rocks; the current was swift and cold and climbing over the wet, slick rocks would be treacherous. Not that way, I thought, not unless a man was absolutely desperate.

Cooking smells drew me back to the center of the camp, making me realize how hungry I was. Except for our "picnic" by the side of the road, I hadn't eaten since the day before. Chickens were roasting over an open fire and I asked Sarge if I could have something to eat.

"I wouldn't like it you didn't ask," he said. "Two was put on for you and the gook lady. There's coffee you want some of that."

I speared two chickens, poured coffee in tin cups, and took everything to the hut where Kim was. She had been dozing sitting up. Now her eyes snapped open and she looked scared.

"Eat," I said, shoving the plate at her. This time there was no bullshit about not wanting the food. She tore off a leg and went to it. "What have you decided? Keep your voice down."

"I've decided to tell the truth."

Her face was expressionless and I couldn't tell what she was thinking. It would be an awful bore if she tried to lay more lies on me.

"That will take some doing." I waited for her to begin.

There was a long pause, then she said "I am part of a resistance group sworn to overthrow the Communist government of this country. You asked Colonel Phuong if there was anti-Communist activity here. There isn't. Not the way you meant. There is a resistance movement, or at least one is forming. At the moment most of our people are in other countries. We have some people here who support us, believe as we do, hate the Communists as much as we do. Soon we will be a force. We will fight back. Our numbers are growing. What we need more than anything is money."

This was hardly what I expected. I let her go on.

"We want no help from the Americans. We wouldn't take it if they offered it. I think they have had enough of Vietnam. All the leaders from the war years are dead or running businesses in the United States. General Ky — President Ky — operates a liquor store in California. He wouldn't be welcome to join us even if he crawled. We want none of the old gang. It was their greed and incompetence plus American stupidity that cost us the war."

I thought of the fifty thousand Americans who had died for her stinking country.

"You Americans could have won, but you weren't ruthless enough."

She took time out from her spiel to gnaw on a chicken leg.

"Never mind that shit. Tell me the rest of it. You expect me to believe you're some kind of freedom fighter? Isn't it a bit late for that?"

She swallowed, and drank a mouthful of bitter coffee. "Of course I expect you to believe me. Forget about everything else I've told you. I'm telling the truth this time. There is a resistance movement and I'm part of it, have been for years. I was in it before I joined the Communist Party and became an agent. My story when they asked me was, I was ashamed of my father and his grafting, the whole rotten middle-class world I lived in. Capitalism I hated like poison, especially American capitalism. I wanted to get back at the Americans for what they had done to my country. Listen to me, Rainey. I believed in my country then and now more than ever. The Communists are destroying it and they have to be stopped. The people must rise up and drive them out. It can be done. I swear it can be done."

I doubted that. Hundreds of thousands of American troops, well trained and superbly equipped—all that and the Air Force—hadn't been able to stop the northern Communists from taking power. But let her talk. Some of what she said might be true.

Now she was tearing the chicken in two; her fingers were greasy. The condemned woman ate a hearty meal, I thought. Albergo had sentenced her to death *in absentia*; it would take some special pleading to make him change his mind.

"We want to return this country to democracy," she continued, sometimes talking with her mouth full. Anxiety can kill the appetite or bring on desperate hunger. Her eyes were bright with patriotic fervor, or what passed for it. The fix she was in seemed to be forgotten as her voice became more emotional. "All over the world there are Vietnamese refugees from Communist terror. I don't mean thieves and grafters but good, honest people who love their country and want to come home. But not to Communist rule. The Communists used guerrilla warfare to take this country. We are going to destroy them using the same methods, Guerrilla tactics. Hit and run. Strike hard and vanish into the mountains and jungles."

"Stick to the point," I said.

"That is the point."

"This group of yours, where's the head office?"

"Los Angeles. But we have people in other cities, other countries. I won't give you the names of our top leaders. I can't do that."

"Skip it. That Chinese hit man I killed, don't tell me you don't know which of us he was after."

"Both of us. His name was Eng and he used to be a member of our group. He betrayed us to the Chinese drug syndicate in Singapore a few weeks before you got here."

"What drug syndicate?"

Her story was so wild, it might just be true. Resistance movements! Drug syndicates! Next week *East Lynne*.

"Our group has been raising money by smuggling heroin into the United States. That's right: heroin. Think what you like. We need the money because what we have isn't enough. What difference does it make, how we get it? America is fucked up anyway. We send heroin and organized crime sends us money."

"And the Chinese syndicate doesn't like that?"

"That's right. The Chinese control, try to control, all the heroin coming from Asia and didn't like anyone else giving them competition. They sent a warning. We ignored it. Our shipments have been small because our supply is limited. We'd smuggle more if we could get it."

"Wonderful. Patriotic heroin. You say this hit man betrayed you. How does a Chinaman get to join a Vietnamese resistance movement?"

"Half Chinese: his father was Vietnamese. Eng was born here and taken to Singapore as a child. Grew up there, made some visits here. In Singapore he was a private detective."

It was getting better. "I knew he smelled of some kind of cop. So he was allowed to join?"

"Eng was still a Vietnamese citizen. Singapore wasn't his real home, he said. He wanted to come back here. He said he hated the Government here because it was persecuting the ethnic Chinese. He was asked how he know about us. He said he was a detective and heard many things. I wasn't there, of course. He joined in Singapore. Some of our people didn't trust him and thought about killing him. Others said he could have sold us to the Communists for money, but hadn't. Our people in Singapore didn't know he was planning to betray them to the syndicate. Not hard to understand: the syndicate pays better."

"Why didn't the syndicate turn you in to the Communists? Gangsters fink on other gangsters all the time.

Kim got up and wiped her hands on a dirty towel that lay beside an equally dirty wash basin. The Georgetown girl was going native. She sat down again.

"I think they were waiting until they knew more about us. Eng never did meet any of our top people. They didn't trust him that much. He gave them what he had and they paid him and told him to continue with us. But we discovered what he had done and put a price on his head. A contract."

"And he heard about it?"

"Yes, word got around as it was supposed to. So he split and went to work for the syndiate." Her story was a loose fit, but it wasn't too bad. Jusst the same, it had a lot of loose threads I didn't like.

"Okay," I said. "So now he's with the opposition. That doesn't explain how he knew about me."

"Go back a few weeks," Kim said. "Eng was still one of us, right? Like the rest of us he heard you had taken a rescue job from Albergo's father. We got the word from our drug buyers in the States. I don't know how they found out. They did. Eng passed on the information to the syndicate. They must have thought that your coming here was a cover for something else. Like Albergo's father was moving into narcotics in a big way.

"Albergo's old man told me he wasn't involved in drugs."

"Maybe the syndicte thought he had changed his mind. You want a surprise? Okay. Albergo's son, this crazy man here, is the syndicate's main supplier in this country. The Chinese don't control the Triangle, he does, and they want it to remain business as usual. If the old man moves in and takes over, that won't be possible. The syndicate wants the son to stay where he is. He hasn't been able to get out because the Chinese won't take him no matter how much money he offers. The reason is, they pay him much less than the market price for heroin. What he gets must be enormous—all these years of doing business, it must be huge—but the money is practically of no use to him. He's a millionaire prisoner."

This was better than a comic book. "The money keeps the government and the military off his back. Why hasn't he bribed his way out?"

"That would be like killing the golden goose." Kim's coffee was gone and she drank some of mine. "The high-ups he pays protection to want to go on collecting. One bribe to smuggle him out and they think perhaps that's the end of the money. Without Albergo this place here will fall apart. Total anarchy. Wholesale killing. Another leader might emerge, but the high-ups Albergo deals with don't want to risk that. They like what they have, why change it?"

I decided to believe her, for all the lurid colors of her story. The fit was getting better and I was ready to buy. Albergo had stayed here all these years because there was no way to get out. The crazy, vicious killer was a prisoner of the Chinese syndicate, the Government grafters, and his own men. A bizarre situation, but there it was; retirement was out of the question, they all wanted him to stay on the job.

What didn't fit was why he finally decided to make a break for it. After all that time, why now? It could be that the stump of his leg had started to rot. He had hinted at that, then told me to mind my own business. But it sounded right now: his leg had been amputated under rough conditions, maybe he needed a second amputation to correct the first. And not getting it, he would certainly die.

I said, "The Chinese must be well armed when their chopper flies in here. Otherwise he could force them to take him out. You ever hear what kind of chopper they use?"

"Our information is they have an American gunship they got at the end of the war."

Why not? You could get your hands on anything after we pulled out. Billions of dollars worth of our stuff stood rotting in the sun. It hadn't been possible to destroy everything.

I said, "They must work it so he can't get close enough to do anything. One guess is, they don't land, just hover. They drop a hook, the heroin goes up, the money comes down. Flying in supplies—food, liquor—is probably part of the deal. Albergo has heavy machine guns and could shoot them down. Then what?"

Kim rubbed her eyes, looking very tired. "What are we going to do, Rainey? Is there any hope at all?"

"I don't know. Albergo wants to talk to me later. I told you why. He may have a plan of his own. He doesn't think much of mine."

"You had a plan?"

"I was going to use you to get us out. Your Government, your credentials."

Her eyes were wary now. "Then you would have to keep me alive?"

"You'd be no good dead."

That didn't satisfy her. "Would you have killed me if you had to?"

"Yes, if I had to. What are you looking so mad about? To me you were an agent working for Colonel Phuong. Were you?"

"Phuong thinks I am. Are you saying our time together would not have meant anything? Killing me wouldn't have bothered you?"

"It would have bothered me. I never did figure you out, but I knew you were dangerous. Slice it any way you like, you were setting me up."

Kim shook her head. "Not for Phuong. I wasn't setting you up. I knew you were going into the Triangle to make contact with Albergo. The rescue story might or might not be true. I had to come along and find out. I told you our people have been sending heroin to the States. But not enough. The Chinese have most of the Vienamese heroin locked up through Albergo. Not just what's grown in here but from other parts of the country. Albergo acts as a warehouse. We thought if we could force out the Chinese, make our own deal with Albergo, then we'd have millions in drug money coming in."

She had been talking fast; now her voice trailed off and she stared at the floor.

"It's all true," she said.

I wasn't about to go easy on her. "You're here, why don't you offer him a deal? Or did you just come along with no clear idea in your head?"

"I thought I could do something."

"And now?"

"Now I'm frightened," she said. "Now I see what he is. He's crazy."

"At least you got that straight," I said. "Tell me, how would your people get the shit out?"

"The same way the Chinese do."

"You think they'd let you?"

"We have more men that they have. My idea was to bring them here to protect Albergo and his operation."

"Why not just kill him and take over?"

"He's been here for years, has established a good working relationship with the poppy farmers, pays them well enough, so they're happy. It takes a long time to get all that going. Besides, our people might not be able to take over. They might find themselves fighting for their lives. Too much fighting and the Government would step in and that would be the end of it. We . . ."

She stopped talking. Someone was coming. Then Sarge's voice boomed out: "Front and center, Rainey! Joe wants to see you. Double-time it, sucker!"

ELEVEN

"WHAT DID she tell you? Did she tell you? Sarge says he didn't hear any rough stuff in there."

Albergo fired off the questions like shots. He was more animated now, brisk and bright-eyed, very much the leader. The bottle of Demerol had been put away, and maybe he had taken a hit of something stronger. I didn't make him for a mainline junkie, but he might be a skin-popper, somebody who injected the heroine under the skin because—according to the drug lore—as long as you could remain at that stage you weren't really an addict.

He had the short-wave radio going: a talk show in Australia. Some guy was phoning in, bitching about the cost of Prince Charlie's last tour. His voice had the tinny sound the callers have on those shows.

I bit the bullet. "She belongs to some resistance group that hope to overturn the Government. Her original story was she got to hate capitalism growing up in America. The I-hate-my-father bit. Very loud about how much she despised America and how much better socialism was. At first radical causes, then the big step when she joined the Communist Party and became an agent for the Viets. Said the FBI and other intelligence were getting too close and she got out fast and came here before they could indict."

"Wait a minute." Albergo went and got a beer. None for me. Whatever he'd been taking had smoothed out the pain lines in his face. No grimaces as he sat back in his chair. "She talked because you said she was going to be killed?"

"I said there might be a chance to save herself."

"How so? If it's there, I don't see it."

"Anything to get her to talk," I said.

"Go on," Albergo said. "Why did she latch onto you? I told you it wouldn't be routine."

I said, "This group she belongs to have been smuggling dope into the States to fund their operation. A lot of money there, but not enough for what they have in mind. A small operation compared to the Singapore syndicate you deal with."

I had hoped to startle him. Didn't work: he remained calm. "She knows about that? Maybe she's just guessing. That's where most of the horse goes before it goes somewhere else."

"She knows. She says you've dealt with them for years. They won't bring you out because you're too profitable where you are."

He didn't like that: violence flickered in his dark eyes. Tell an ordinary man what he doesn't want to hear and you may incur his enmity. Tell a paranoid and you may be risking sudden death.

He got a hold on himself. "What else?"

175

"She knew I was coming here because their drug buyers in the States heard about the job and passed the word. Your father doesn't deal in dope. These people decided maybe he was getting ready to. She doesn't know the story there. Nobody likes serious competition. Maybe the dope territories are all fixed and there's no room for a newcomer."

Albergo pointed the empty bottle at me. "Don't waste time talking about what you don't know. I want to know what was in that cunt's head."

"She said you were only getting middle dollar from the Chinese. Her group can't get enough horse and would pay much more than you're getting. For steady supply. She came up here with me, to see what was happening and maybe make a deal—if you could break off with the syndicate."

Albergo threw the bottle on the floor. "I can break off any time I like. You see what I have here. You think the slopes want to go up against that? Shit! I think she's just jerking you off."

"She says they come to pick up the shit with a gunship. How can she know that? Do they?"

"Yeah, they have a gunship. Never mind that. You seem to think this broad is valuable. Why is that?"

"No matter how we go out of here there's a lot of country to be crossed before we're safe. If she's telling the truth—I think she is—her group has contacts everywhere. That's better than flying blind. Kill her and you lose that advantage."

"You don't want to kill her anyway."

"I'd just as soon not kill her. Maybe I have a soft spot for her."

"You have a soft spot for her soft spot," Albergo said. No smile. "Just as long as you don't step on your dick, I don't care what you have. All right, so she goes on living for a while longer. We'll use her after we get out. How do we get out? That first plan of yours is shit. Can't work, won't work, it's shit! You really think we could have driven down half the country with a gun in the cunt's back?"

"How could I make a better plan? I didn't know what was going on here."

Albergo got another beer. None for me. "We've been over all that. Don't make excuses. My old man promises to pay you two hundred grand and that's the best you can do?"

I didn't sense any threat in his little outburst. The cripple berating the whole man; that's all it was. He opened his mouth, held the bottle up, and let the beer spill out while he swallowed fast. The dumber GI's do that. Albergo was full of weird moves.

"If we could take the chopper," I said. "Kill everybody but the pilot, we could fly out of here."

"You think I haven't thought of that? Just like that! Take the chopper and fly out."

"Not just like that," I said. "I figure they never land here. They come in and hover, hold the chopper steady while the swap is made. Dope goes up, money comes down, then they fly away. You have firepower, they have as much or more. Yeah, you could bring them down, the way your heavy stuff is set up. Them maybe you'd be stuck here forever."

Cold anger smoldered in his dark eyes; who could tell what went on in that festering mind of his? In all probablity here was a man who hated every living thing. Even Eichmann loved his wife. This guy loved nothing, least of all himself.

"Nothing is forever," he said.

"It could feel like forever, in here," I said.

"How would you take this chopper? For a big man you have a small brain. Here on the ground I have a lot of men that don't want me to leave. I can understand that even if you can't. I hold them together, make money for them, fix it so Government troops aren't air-lifted in here to kill them. They could fight, they couldn't win. Captured, they'd be shot. Business with the syndicate is an ongoing thing because of me. Okay, the cunt is right, they only pay me middle dollar but that's still a lot of money. The men get their share and there isn't a guy in here isn't rich. All that is on the plus side, with one big difference: they can't get out, they can't go back home or somewhere else and live like Arab oil sheiks or pop stars. And because they can't do it— here's the point—the don't want anybody else to do it. They'll try to kill me before they'll let that happen."

"Kill them first," I said. "I have a new plan. You want to hear it?"

"It better not be as dumb as the first one."

Outwardly menacing, he was less hostile now. Letting down his guard wasn't possible for him, but he was interested, he was listening. Killing the men had occurred to him; he hadn't been able to figure out how it could be used to make his escape. Which was understandable since his only back-up was Sarge, a tough man but not bright man, and as he knew and I knew, he might not have Sarge.

"It can work if it's done right. Up till now it's been a standoff between you and the Chinese. Year after year it's been like that: they collect and pay off. In ten years how much profit have they made? Billions. You have any real trouble with them?"

Albergo shook his head, not liking to be questioned but accepting the need for an answer. "There was a time when I liked it here. Last year I asked them to bring me out, offered them big money to do it, really big money. They said no. I upped the offer, said I would throw in the next shipment as part of the deal, even offered to work with them when I got back home. They wouldn't go for it. I haven't asked since then."

"Then your business with them has been trouble free. You're a sound client who doesn't rock the boat. We have to rock the boat, shake them up. Suddenly after so much time, the operation here—suddenly—is all fucked up. They don't panic, but they're concerned. First we kill the men because it has to be done. But there's more to it. We get rid of the bodies, put them in the caves, then we burn the huts and wreck every piece of equipment in here."

Albergo's eyes bore into me. "This better be going somewhere."

I said, ignoring the warning, "We make it

179

look like this place has come under air attack. After we kill the men we use the machine guns to scar up the cliffs with bullets. You have explosives?"

He nodded.

"We set them off here and there to make it look like rocket hits. We napalm all round, even up at the top of the cliffs. Total destruction."

"We don't have any fucking napalm."

"We make it out of gasoline and motor oil," I went on. "You have kerosene for the lamps, so we mix that in. What we get will burn much the same. After we get through this place will look as if it's been zapped."

"Then what?" Albergo's hands were motionless on the arms of his chair. He was starting to catch on.

"You get on the radio to the Chinese and tell them you're coming under heavy air attack and are evacuating. Going out the back way where the river comes in. They know about that?"

"They can see it, can't they? When they fly in. Yeah, they know about it."

"You tell them you're taking off, will take the radio and get back to them later when you find another place in the mountains. They'll want to know how soon. You don't know. Later is later. A new place may be hard to find. Then you switch off and they're talking to radio silence."

Albergo patted the arm of the chair with both hands. His eyes seemed to be turned inward. I waited.

"Why would they come here at all?" he said finally. "I see what you're getting at, but if I tell them the place has been clobbered, why would they risk coming up against Government choppers, maybe MIG's? Why wouldn't they wait to hear from me?"

I said, "They'll wait for a while, give you time to get set up again, give the Government choppers—whatever—time to get out of this area. They don't hear from you, they'll come."

"How are you so fucking sure of that?"

"Where would you start if you were looking for somebody? In the last place they were, right? They'll want to check out if you were telling the truth and not working some double cross. They'll want to see for themselves. There's too much money involved for them not to come. They'll be careful, sure. Don't except them to just fly in here and land. First they'll make a few low passes to see what it looks like down here. They'll see what's been set up for them to see. Then finally they'll come in here and set down."

"Why are you so sure?" he repeated. "They may want a closer look, but why do they have to land?"

"They get in so close, nothing is moving, no bodies, nothing. Nobody is shooting at them, all they see is devastation, why wouldn't they land? Curiosity, maybe. But the people they work for will want to know for sure. Is there any unrefined heroin left here? It bulks bigger than pure. Some of it could be left. When you talk on the radio you're going to tell them you're going out with nothing but small arms. Everything else has to be abandoned."

"Okay, so they'll probably land the chopper.

They're not so dumb they'll all jump down and walk around checking the ruins. That thing has two gunners. You can bet your ass they won't leave the ship. The two other slopes, the money men, they'll probably walk around, not the gunners, not even if this place is like the grave. The pilot—remember him—won't budge from his seat."

Everything he said was right on the button; they would do it like that. Albergo stared at me, knowing I was onto something good, also knowing that here was the toughest part of the operation. I knew it too.

"The gunners will be covering the money men," I told him. "We have to come up fast from behind."

Albergo shifted his metal leg. "Yeah, we'll run like the wind."

"We'll come up from behind and blow them away," I said. "Pilots are usually just pilots. I don't see any real trouble there. We take the chopper and fly out. Where to I don't know. We'll talk to the pilot."

"Why don't you want to leave bodies when we zap this place? I would think that would make it look more real."

"No. Nobody has to be here when they come. Not even bodies. You didn't put up a fight. What fight? Against choppers? You heard them coming over and you took off, leaving everything behind. In a situation like that nothing else would make sense. You got out with all your men. Now you're somewhere in the mountains."

Albergo got to his feet and went to the box where the beer was. "You want one?" he asked.

We drank beer and I waited for his decision. I figured he would say yes, but with crazies how can you be sure? Going out by chopper was the only way open; by now Colonel Phuong's men might have found the taxi driver, the Chinese assassin's wheels, and got him to talk. From there it was just a step linking Kim to the resistance movement. Even now, there might be soldiers and security men heading in to the mountains.

"I'll be up shit creek if this doesn't work," Albergo said. Then he remembered that now we were beer drinking buddies and he changed it to: "Both of us will be up shit creek. The broad I don't care about. You don't want to kill her, we won't kill her."

"She'll be an extra gun."

"Yeah, there's that. The VC gook women were good shots. This broad could be. I'm thinking about Sarge."

"You think you can trust him?"

"Probably. He's good man for a nigger. A lot of times I had to depend on Sarge and he always came through. No genius, he does what he's told. Once or twice when I was sick he could have took over. But he didn't. He stayed with me. He doesn't want to leave here. I can see that, in a way. We have a kind of community going here. Life is simple if you make it simple. There's not so much shit in here as there is out there."

Albergo waved his beer bottle, indicating the outside world. "Sarge won't want to go but he'll have to. Not to the States unless he makes it in through Canada or Mexico. But he doesn't want to go back even if he didn't have charges hanging over him."

"Better not give him too much time to think about it."

183

"Yeah, he might get confused."

"How much time do we have before the next pickup?"

"Two weeks, This is the last month in the third quarter of the year. Usually they're on time. Sometimes they're a few days early, a few days late. When that happens, they use the radio."

"Then we may have less than two weeks."

"Make it two weeks. The schedule has been met for over a year. Get two more beers, will you?"

I got them.

Albergo's voice was casual; nothing in his tone suggested that he was talking about the lives of men he had known for years. Getting rid of them would be a service to humanity, not that I thought about it in such lofty terms. They had to be killed before they could kill. But if there had been any other way, I would have let them live out their stinking lives.

"We have to get them all together," I said. "A funeral would do it. Anybody sick enough to die?"

"No. Even if they were it wouldn't mean anything. In here we don't blow Taps and fire off rifles. A guy dies he gets put in a hole and covered over. The faggot weddings are something else. These faggots do get married. Bobby, that junkie Sarge killed, was married to Buck, the guy that buried him. Felt guilty probably. Sarge did him a favor, gave him a shotgun divorce. Now he can marry that Cambodian kid he's got the hots for. A mean bastard, that Cambodian, but Buck can't get enough of his ass."

Albergo broke off to stare at me.

"Are you thinking the same thing I'm thinking?"

"Yeah. A faggot wedding. When was the last one?"

"Months ago. Guys stayed drunk for days, all but the lookouts. Any excuse will do. Not good for security, but you can't keep them under too tight discipline. This time we'll go whole hog with the celebrating. This time, no lookouts. Everybody gets to join in the fun. We'll catch them at the height of the festivities. I can see it. It'll be a slaughter."

"Who does the marrying? You?"

"A hillbilly that used to be a child evangelist performs the ceremony. The fuckers seem to think it's legal, I don't know why. I'm beginning to feel better about this whole thing. Putting them together was the next to biggest problem. Now I can't see how we can miss. Funny how if you kick something around with another guy you come up with the right answer. I'm glad you're in this with me, Rainey."

Albergo's attempt to be friendly was so false, so difficult and out of character, that I wanted to smile. I thought of the old Texas saying, and it certainly applied here: "I'd drother eat off the same plate as a snake as be friends with that feller." But I grunted my appreciation of the compliment.

"How soon can we get them married?" I asked.

"Tomorrow," Albergo said. "That soon enough for you?"

"The sooner, the better."

"I'll get it on early. The guys will jump at the chance to celebrate. Life can get dull in here. A noon wedding, I think. Buck and the Cambodian. Dirty cocksuckers! Marry them at noon and there will be the whole afternoon to get drunk. Then after they're dead we have two weeks to get set."

Whatever Albergo was taking was wearing off; his face was a bad color. This was a very sick man. He was sweating more than he should have been.

"That should do it. Fucking malaria comes back every year. Atabrine doesn't help much. I've got to lie down for a while. Go back to the broad. Take off now. See you in the morning."

It was getting dark when I went back to Kim; a kerosene lamp on a table gave off dull, yellow light. Sarge was nowhere to be seen. Men were cooking over open fires and there was the smell of cooking meat and woodsmoke. Through the open window came the rippling sound of the river running over rocks.

Kim had been lying on a cot. She got up when I came in.

"How did it go?" she said. "What did you tell him?"

"What you told me. Hear me out. It worked. I think he's half convinced you can help us later. I told him you have people everywhere."

"Where is everywhere?" Kim gave me a weak smile.

"Good question. Where do we go from here?"

Kim said nothing. She was sitting on the cot with her legs drawn up. Her arms were wrapped around her knees, as if trying to hug herself. Women often do that when they're

186

depressed or afraid. She had every reason to be both.

"You'll have to take part in it," I said after I told her about the fag wedding and how it was going to end.

She took it calmly enough. I thought she might have balked at participating in mass killing.

"All right," she said.

"Ever fire an automatic rifle?"

"Yes. AK-47's, M-16's, even the AKM."

"Can't do better than that," I said.

The AKM was the current army rifle of the USSR, an improved version of the AK-47, and that's saying something. It had the same 600 rpm rate of fire, the same 30 round magazine, the same 7.62 mm caliber. No better assault rifle in the world.

"You'll be okay," I said. "It should be a piece of cake. Most of them will be drunk. A few won't want to drink that much. Not many though. The sober ones get it first. We open up and pour it on. It can't become a firefight. We have to kill everybody. A few men—if they got away—could give us a bad time, sniping from the cliffs. You think you're a tough broad. Are you? You can't start throwing up if some guy comes running at you with his guts hanging out. You have to look good when the killing starts."

Kim stared at me, hugging her knees and shivering a little, though it wasn't cold. I didn't set much store by her contacts on the outside. The higher-ups of this so-called resistance movement might be using people like her to get rich. Or she might have her own ideas along that line.

"What's the matter?" I said.

A little shrug for an answer. Then she said, "You haven't made a deal behind my back, have you? Use me as an extra rifle and then let Albergo kill me?"

"You can't be that good with a rifle."

"Good enough, you'll see. What about Sarge?"

"Albergo has counted him in for now. What should I do? Question his judgement?"

"I'm afraid of Sarge," Kim said.

"Be more afraid of Albergo. He's the one to watch."

"He'll be bringing out a lot of money?"

I had given some thought to that. No business of mine how much he took out unless he had it stashed in six big suticases. Excess baggage that could get in the way. It was the heroin that bothered me. Call me a square if you like, but I couldn't go along with that. Millions in cash he was sure to have and every cent of it had been made from human misery. Nothing could be done to change that. No heroin, though: I wouldn't let him bring heroin, refined or unrefined, back to the States. I'd kill him first. I might have to.

"You interested in his money?" I asked her.

"He looks like he's dying, to me."

"What are you now? A doctor? You think you're going to be mentioned in his will. Maybe you think we can kill the men, then kill Albergo and Sarge, then take the chopper and fly off into the sunset. Music up, right?"

Her answer was surprisingly simple. Actually it was a question. "Why not?" she said.

I said, "Why not is we can't take the chopper without them. Why not is I didn't come here

188

to kill the man and then steal his dirty money. And last but not least—you bet your ass, not least—is I'd be next on your hit list. I know what you patriots are like. Anything for a cause, no matter how shitty."

A foxy lady, this one; not ready to drop it just yet. Some people are like that. They're hanging over the edge of a thousand-foot glacier and you're on the other end of the rope and they still want to talk deals.

"I wouldn't turn on you," she said. "Not after all we've been through."

"You think we've been through a lot? You think that then you don't know what's coming up. We have a plan, right? Doesn't look too bad, and instead of being glad maybe you have a chance you want to do in Albergo and maybe me."

Sincerity was her middle name; travel the world and you'd find it hard to find someone so sincere.

"I was thinking fifty-fifty shares," she said.

Here, even in this most dangerous situation, she interested me.

"What makes you think you're entitled to anything?"

"I thought...Well, we're together in this, aren't we?"

"I'm together with myself," I said. But I smiled when I said it. Time comes when things are so bad, so ridiculous, there's nothing else you can do.

Kim gave me a sad smile. There was more reproach than condemnation in it.

"I'm sorry to hear that, Rainey."

"I'm going to sleep. You want to come along?"

189

Kim put her feet on the floor, unsmiling now, but interested. "You want me to?"

I said, "Just as long as you don't talk business."

As it turned out, we didn't.

TWELVE

I WOKE up to wild laughter, some cheering, and went to the window in time to see Albergo and a bunch of the men going up the hill to where the base of the cliff was pocked with caves. One of the deepest caves was a sort of strong room fitted with a heavy steel gate set in bored-out rock. The gate was chained and padlocked, and it was more a deterrent then anything else; Albergo wanted the men to know the cave wasn't a candy store. I knew there was heroin in there, and supplies, and maybe even money.

They went in and came out carrying bottles of liquor, Albergo doing his sour best to get into the festive mood, the men kidding around, wanting to get at the booze. Wedding bells, I thought. We are gathered here today to join in holy matrimony...

It wasn't hard to figure who was going to do the marrying. Up the hill came a gangling hick who was still a hick in spite of his native shirt and conical hat. The men jeered but he didn't jeer back, didn't even crack a smile. The child evangelist: they have them in our Southland;

they have them even in the Golden Triangle.

They went down with the preacher trailing behind, a Bible in one hand, a bottle in the other. He looked crazy and probably was crazy. I wondered why he hadn't been able to beat the draft. Nearly ten years after the war, none of them was all that young; this guy had the slouching gait and the mindless eyes of an innocent idiot child.

Rubbing her eyes, on the cot, Kim wanted to know what the noise was about.

"Oh Jesus!" she said when I told her.

"Get dressed," I said.

By the time we went down to the river to wash, Buck and the Cambodian weasel were surrounded by members of the wedding and every one had a bottle. When the fat Guamian saw Kim he made a sucking sound and said to Albergo, "Hey there, boss, how's about lettin' me marry dat?"

Albergo laughed like a rusty hinge and yelled back, not too convincingly, "Put that in writing, Jelly Belly. Hey Rainey," he called to me. "Are you ready for this? Buck and The Street Fighter are getting married. You and your girlfriend got to help us celebrate."

"Be right up," I said.

Down at the shallow river, splashing water in her face, Kim said, "You think this is going to work?"

"It's going to work," I told her. "There's no set plan. When it looks right, we'll do it. Albergo will get behind a .30 caliber. We'll have sixteens. Sarge will be on shotgun. Can't use grenades because we'll be too close. A few minutes, it should be quiet here."

Kim dried her face with her shirt, then out it on.

No longer marked for execution, she was more confident now. Her eyes, always a little hard, were harder, and her entire manner was determined. Nothing more was said about wasting Albergo, which didn't mean she wasn't thinking about it.

It was still early enough to be only moderately hot; most of Albergo City was still in shadow. Up where the party was, in the bare brown space between the huts, this lawless settlement's village square, rough tables had been set up and on them were bottles and glasses and a lot of canned food. The syndicate might insist on keeping Albergo a prisoner, but they didn't want him to go hungry. Laid out for the guests was the sort of stuff you see in gourmet shops in the States: chicken, ham, smoked oysters, caviar, salmon, cocktail sausages—all brought down from the cave with the barred door. A suitcase radio provided music and some of the goons were dancing. It was a sight that would have gladdened a caterer's heart.

Albergo was having a few just to be sociable, but I could tell he didn't like the stuff. We were introduced to the bridal pair and Sarge gave us drinks. The look he gave me told me he was in on it; no problem there. Not all but most of the men were wearing sidearms, nothing heavier than that.

We were breakfasting on watered whiskey and smoked oysters on crisps when the fat Guamian came over and asked Kim to dance. She looked at me and I nodded.

193

"Dance with the guy," I said.

Albergo was a few feet away and he said, "No ass grabbing, Jelly Belly. You get excited, go beat the meat."

A man of refinement, you have to admit that; I didn't mind as long as he kept his word about Kim. The Guamian, a brown tub of guts, didn't like the warning, but wasn't ready to be insubordinate to his commanding officer.

Albergo came over to me. "It's eight-oh-five now. They should be drunk by noon. We'll give them a little longer. Some will be passed out by then, some will be getting there, a few will be waking up looking for more booze. I'll open up with the closest .30. That's your signal."

"Our weapons are where?"

"Sarge put them on your bed while you were at the river. Under the blanket. Grope the broad. Make it look like you're going up there to tear off a piece. You and the bitch better be ready."

"We'll be ready. How about Sarge?"

Albergo looked at where Sarge was standing with the white-bearded Frenchman. They were clinking glasses and laughing like bastards. The Frenchman had two USAF .38's stuck in the waistband of his pants. Sarge carried the combat shotgun in a sling. No sidearm that I could see. I guess Sarge carried the Savage all the time and nobody even thought about it. He was wearing a camouflage jacket and the pockets bulged with shells. Good old Sarge, always ready for emergencies.

"You see him, don't you?" Albergo said. "He thinks he's going out with us."

I looked again. "Isn't he?"

"Well nothing is for sure, is it?" Albergo walked away before I could ask any more questions.

It didn't seem to occur to him that Sarge and the men dead he'd be alone with all his heroin, all his money. If he didn't think he could handle me, then it had to be trust in my reputation, passed along by his old man. An odd feeling, to be trusted by someone like Joe Albergo, Jr.

The morning wore on and the party got wilder. Now it was hot but not too bad in the shadow of the great cliff. This was the first time I'd seen all the men together; I began to count. I got to thirty one and added in the three men still behind the machine guns that covered the road coming down into the gorge. Albergo would get behind the gun closest to the wedding party. The gunners hadn't been called down yet.

I was thinking about that when Albergo turned, cupped his hands and shouted above the noise of the blaring rock music. "Hey you guys, get your asses down here—this is a party! Front and center, you mothers!"

The members of the wedding yelled too, even the getting-old Frenchman. Everybody was laughing and having a good time. Long free of the Guamian and six or seven of the others, Kim was eating spiced meat off a tin plate. She asked me to fix her a drink and I made it tall and watery and her eyes snapped when she tasted it.

I grinned at her. "Tonight you can get smashed."

I wondered what she was thinking; could be

195

high finance or the very real possibility that she would be killed inside of an hour or so. An ambush isn't always a success and if they managed to get off a few rounds, one of those rounds might find her. Same thing went for the rest of us, though it might not be such a bad thing if Albergo got his. No way to know how Sarge would take it, if it happened. I'd just have to be ready for it.

The gunners came down from the guns and drank hard because they had a lot of catching up to do. Allowing for differences, it was much like a party anywhere. It had its showoffs and its wallflowers, its laughers and its depressives. The one weeper turned out to be the fat and extremely dangerous Guamian. Not everyone danced. Albergo couldn't dance and Sarge didn't. I did my special box rumba with Kim to show I wasn't a party poop. And the sounds of merriment rolled up into the pitiless blue sky.

Albergo looked at his watch and Sarge hit the bottom on the transistor. The preacher, mired in theological gloom, jerked to his feet and whacked his bible with his free hand. It was the first time I'd seen anyone actually thump a bible.

"Gather round, brothers and sisters," the padre commanded. "It's time to get on with the ceremony."

The Frenchman gave the bride away; Sarge was best man. A simple ceremony in spite of its barbarian trappings. Nobody cried except the fat Guamian. The preacher sounded like my part of the country, though I hate to admit it. He sounded like one of those old timey

196

country singers who "talked" their songs. It was like one of those cold-sweat dreams rummies have when they're going through alcohol withdrawal.

"You may now kiss the bride," the preacher concluded.

"Where the fuck do you think you're going?" Albergo said when the bride and groom started for their hut. "You been going at it all night— the honeymoon can wait." Then he softened it with, "Stay a while, kids, or you'll miss the reception."

Albergo raised the bottle he'd been nipping from. "A toast to the bride and groom! May all their troubles be little ones!"

The sinister son of a bitch!

An hour later Buck was snoring in The Street Fighter's arms. The Cambodian was nodding with a bottle in his hand. Now and then he let a little whiskey trickle into Buck's mouth. Five couples were stumbling through a dance. About fifteen of the guests lay unconscious on the bare earth; the rest were sitting or standing or hunkered down, some drinking, some not, but all bleary-eyed with booze. Albergo looked at me and I looked at Kim. Then we edged off to the hut, her hand on my ass, mine on hers. Snapping his fingers, digging the music, Sarge wandered off down the slope to the river.

We got inside and found the M-16's, the clips to go with them. Kim's face was the color of putty. I squeezed her arm and she pulled away from me.

"Fuck off," she hissed.

Albergo was getting behind the gun when we got to the door. He saw us and he nodded. I couldn't see Sarge from where we were. We had the bolts pulled on the sixteens. The music kept on blaring. Somebody yelled in an excess of high spirits.

And Albergo opened fire.

A funny thing: coming out in front of Kim I saw he was wearing glasses. The mind is like that. Then I forgot about Albergo and we moved in on them firing the sixteens. Albergo got most of the dancers within seconds. Then he got the rest. Sarge was moving in steady but fast and the slide-action Savage boomed in his hands. I blew away the men at the tables with a long burst from the sixteen, and then turned it on the men who were trying to get up off the ground. The .30 caliber kept on chattering, louder than it would have been in open country.Sarge reloaded as he walked and the Savage started booming again. Men were screaming, some trying to run. Then I realized that the loudest screaming was coming from Kim. She screamed as she rattled bullets through the sixteen, getting in closer than she should, ignoring me when I yelled at her to hold back. Some return fire was coming at us. It was weak and scattered and wasn't doing any good. It faltered and died.

And then suddenly it was over except that Albergo was still firing the .30 caliber, sweeping it back and forth across the bullet-chewed clearing, shredding bodies already dead. It went on and on, the relentless chatter of the .30 caliber. Then it stopped and we moved in, raking the clearing with our own fire. A man groaned and Sarge blew his head off. That part of the gorge smelled of smoke and overheated weapons and the ground was splashed with blood and liquor.

No one moved. Albergo came limping down the slope, the .45 in his hand, no expression on his face. I wondered if Sarge's moment had come. I thought I'd probably kill Albergo if he raised the .45 and pointed it in any direction. But nothing happened.

"Some marriages aren't meant to last," he said. No smile. "Take ten, then move the bodies like we planned. You were right, Rainey. It worked like a charm."

I knew his old man would have been proud of him. Even Big Al would have been proud, and maybe a little envious. After all, Big Al's biggest score at one time was seven dummies on Valentine's Day.

"It got done," I said.

"You were good too," he said to Kim.

"Thanks," she said.

"That's right." Albergo remembered that he still had his glasses on. He grimanced with embarrassment and put them in his shirt pocket. There was another pair in the other pocket. I hadn't seen them before because his shirt had been buttoned. A single bottle had been left intact and Kim and I drank from it and the Sarge drank, but not Albergo.

The hot wind blew away the smells of the battle and the river ran over the rocks. It was nice to be dead. Sarge was in good humor and he drank off enough whisky to make another man drunk. All it did to him was make him grim and snap his fingers.

Now we were comrades together: four against the world. Yeah!

Albergo didn't help with the bodies, which

was understandable. Look at it this way: he was the boss and he was missing a leg. So he sat at one of the tables and drank river water while we did the work.

And if you haven't done it, you better believe moving thirty four dead men can be an awful lot of work. Especially when it's just past noon in the tropics and it's all uphill. We used the jeeps and got our hands and clothes bloody. Everybody sweated. Getting them up the hill and into the cave took two hours and then it was time for a well-earned rest.

We took it, then started the destruction bit an hour later.

I could tell by the look on Sarge's face that he didn't like wrecking all that good equipment. But like the old soldier he was, he followed orders. We positioned the jeeps and used grenades on them. Then, sweating like pigs, Sarge helped me place the explosives and we set them off. That started fires in the dry grass and brush and when it burned out and the smoke cleared and we could see, it looked pretty good, with deep holes that might have been made by rocket hits all along the center of the gorge and some along the bank of the river.

It took longer to burn the huts that were meant to burn that day. If we burned them all together we'd suffocate because the gorge was narrow and the wind had died down. Albergo just sat and drank water while this was going on.

It was getting dark when we finished that part of it, with a lot more to be done on the following day.

Albergo went to his hut; Sarge to his own. Kim and I got clean suntans and went down to the river to get cleaned up. Darkness comes fast in the tropics and even with a moon it was hard to see at the bottom of the gorge. Everything still smelled of smoke and explosives. It might have been romantic, splashing naked in an Asian river, if not for that.

We went to bed with only enough energy left to do it once.

Albergo was an insomniac or he liked to get up early. The plan to grab the chopper was my idea, but he had taken it over and was pushing us hard.

"Rise and shine!" he yelled, beating on something metal.

I pulled on my pants and found him, shaved and sallow, whacking the hood of a mangled jeep with a stick.

He looked worse now and I didn't think it was just a recurrent attack of malaria. Maybe Kim was right. Maybe he was dying.

"Let's get this show on the road," he said, remote and irritable. "You and Sarge take a gun up top and scar up the cliffs like you said. Then you can eat."

We shot up the cliffs before breakfast, using up a lot of ammunition, and after we dined on coffee and leftovers from the party, it was time to start mixing the homemade napalm.

Napalm has got to be the most vicious shit in the world. What it can do to the human body is the stuff of nightmares. Back when they were first using it, it came in jellied form. These days it's a slimy liquid and burns hotter and has better adhesive qualities. Science is always aiming for better things.

We mixed gasoline, kerosene, and motor oil in oil drums, then filled twenty-four gas cans, all we had, and set them, two at a time, in various parts of the gorge. Sarge exploded some with rifle fire. I took care of the others. What was left in the oil drum we poured into two five-gallon glass jugs, then took them to the top of the cliff, one final touch in our phony napalm attack. Sarge threw them out far and I blew them up with M-16 bullets. Each time the bullets hit there was a bright yellow flash, hardly any noise as the fiercely burning slop splattered all over the cliff on the other side of the gorge. It trickled down flaming and oily and we both agreed the effect was pretty good.

From the top of the cliff the gorge did look as if it had come under heavy air attack.

"The syndicate slopes see that, they have to be convinced," Sarge said.

I hoped he was right.

After that there wasn't a whole lot to do except to seal up the mouth of the cave where the bodies were, to keep them from stinking. Turning the gorge into a war zone took another day. That night I tried to talk to Albergo about going ahead with the plan. He said he wasn't ready. There still were a few things to think about. He was in his hut, lying on his cot, his metal leg unfastened and lying under the blanket beside him. His face was white and he was sweating, Asking him if he needed help would have sent him into a rage, so I didn't do it.

"Tomorrow we'll get on it," was all I could get

out of him.

Sarge was drunk and singing in his hut. Kim was drinking whisky and listening to a transistor radio when I went back to our digs.

"How is the great man tonight?" she wanted to know. "Is it a go or isn't it?"

"Not right now it isn't. Guy is sick. We may have to do it without him, load him on board after it's done. If he has enough dope in him he won't know what's happening."

Kim smiled maliciously. "If he takes enough dope he'll die."

"You're back to that shit?"

Kim splashed whisky in her glass and drank it off. There was a wildness about her that made me wonder if she might not try to take out all of us, then try for the chopper. She had more moods than a mood ring, and even if she got out of this, I didn't see a long life ahead of her.

"What if I am back to it?" she said. "You have the chance of a lifetime here and for some stupid reason you don't want to take it. What the hell is wrong with you? You don't have to believe what I believe. All you have to do is take your half and go your way. This soldier of fortune thing you do, how long do you think that's going to last? Why should it last when it doesn't have to?"

"You're asking for it."

"What can you do? Shoot me?"

"I can slap you silly."

I made a move toward her and her hand went down to the bunched up blankets and came up holding an Air Force Smith & Wesson .38. I hadn't seen her hide it when we collected

203

the weapons from among the dead.

"Try it, Rainey."

My pal, my bedmate. I didn't want to get shot just because she wanted to talk. The money and the heroin were beginning to obsess her.

I sat down well away from her. "Let us not get carried away," I said. "We're close to getting out of this. Mess up a little and you'll mess up a lot."

"You're the mess. It's because time is short we have to settle this. You say it's settled. Like hell! You say you're together with yourself. So all right, be a horse's ass. But I'm entitled to a share and I'm going to get it."

"Think what you like. It's not going to work out that way."

"That's what you think."

"What'll you do? Shoot me?"

"You're a fool and you're getting in the way of something bigger than you are. That money and the heroin could mean a new life for my country. It would be a start. I didn't live in America for nothing. It takes money to make money."

I was mad enough to say, "Sure, it was the money-grubbing Yankees that corrupted your wonderful government. Ah, forget it. This conversation is a lot of shit. I'm going to bed."

She raised the .38. "I haven't finished yet. I'm asking you to give us a chance. Rainey."

"You always point a gun when you ask favors?"

Drunk or not, she knew she was on the bad side of me and might not get back. These broads! Even these Viet broads! They think they can switch it on and off. The charm is what I mean.

Now it was switched on again. "I'd never do anything bad to you, Rainey. The gun . . . here, take it!"

She held it out, butt toward me.

"Keep it," I told her. "Listen, okay? You wouldn't shoot me. So let's not go on about it. But that changes nothing. You can't have the fucking heroin."

"Can I have the money? It's obvious you don't want it."

Round and round the mulberry bush. I said, "We're not going to kill Albergo to take his money. We're not going to kill him for any reason."

She put the gun down and drank some whisky. I have no statistics on how many women alcoholics there are in Vietnam. Probably not many. This one could be setting a new trend.

"I'm sure he intends to kill us," she said. "Albergo and the black man intend to kill us as soon as they have the helicopter."

"That is very unsporting of them."

She wasn't telling me anything I hadn't thought about. They would need my gun to take the chopper. After it was over they might see me as a fifth wheel at best; a threat at worst. And I had had a few deep thoughts about the lady I was talking to.

"Stale wisecracks won't do it, Rainey."

Then she remembered that she had to get back on my good side. I was her friend, remember? Without me, she'd be catfood for these two guys. If she didn't believe that, then she was a fool.

"Let's wait and see," I said. "Where's that oriental patience I'm always hearing about? How does it go: 'Wait long enough by the river and the body of your enemy will float by.' "

Kim's smile had daggers in it. "Go to bed, Rainey. You're drunk and you haven't even been drinking."

I lay down on the other cot with my eyes closed. Now and then I heard the glass and bottle. I could see her: this kid wasn't faking it, she was psyching herself up to do something. Silly bitch! As if she thought she could get away with it.

She called me nasty names in a whisper. But I think there was some affection there too. They say love never really dies. They say liking lasts longer than love. They say a lot of things. Down yonder in his hut, Sarge was singing. That 'ol boy sure liked to sing when he got a load on. Being so big, so hardened to the stuff, his kind of load would take three men to carry.

No sounds from Albergo's cottage. He always kept the radio switched on, ready to receive, but from his short wave there wasn't a peep. Kim was asleep, passed out in the chair.

To make sure, I reached down for a boot and dropped it. No reaction, not even a nervous twitch. I got up and took the USAF .38, pushed open the cylinder, spilled the rounds on the blanket. It took a long time to work the lead out of the casings. I dusted out the powder onto a piece of paper, then I worked the lead back in. Then I blew the powder away. I wasn't leaving her defenseless: she wouldn't be using a handgun when the Singapore chinks came flying in.

flying in.

I covered her with a blanket before I sacked out for the rest of the night.

THIRTEEN

WE WERE as ready as we would ever be.

Albergo was dying on his feet—it had to be gangrene—but he kept going. I figured he was using Demerol and speed, maybe even heroin and speed. I couldn't be sure about gangrene, but whatever it was, it was killing him. There was no smell yet; that would come soon.

Albergo said he wasn't sure where the syndicate chopper came from. He thought it was some isolated village just over the Laotian border. It certainly couldn't come from Singapore. He said they might be flying the heroin out by plane from some airstrip in Laos or, not too likely, smuggling in aboard a cargo ship on the South China Sea coast of Vietnam.

All that was for later: the pilot would tell us when we grabbed him.

They were using an assault helicopter with a lot of heavy stuff on it: rockets, cannon, heavy machine guns. It was armored so it could fight in the air if it had to. That wouldn't do much good if we were spotted. It would be better than being captured.

For reasons of his own, Albergo had been stalling for days. Maybe he knew he was dying and wanted to die where he had ruled for so long. If I found myself in a fix like that I would drink some whisky and then shoot myself. I *think* that's what I would do. But we can't know what we're going to do until it's time to do it. Everybody goes out in his own way.

Then early one morning he came out of his hut and told us to get ready. I had allowed him to keep on giving orders only because of Sarge. The big black man would not take orders except when they were relayed through Albergo. We were too close to the end to start fighting. Any fight with Sarge was a fight to the finish.

We ate breakfast. Albergo ate nothing. He limped around, using the cane, a bottle of beer always in his hand. Not the best medicine for gangrene, but it hardly made any difference. Sarge had been drinking the night before and he was sullen and red-eyed. He stared at the walls of the gorge, at the river, at the burned huts. Poor guy, he was being forced to leave his happy home and he didn't like it.

We burned two of the last three huts, leaving Albergo's intact until he raised his syndicate contacts on the radio. He sat at the radio and he got them with no trouble at all, which reinforced his idea that the pick-up chopper was based at no great distance. The accentless Chinese voice was as clear as if it had been coming from the next room.

"Identify yourself! Identify yourself!" the voice said.

"This is Happy Dreams," Albergo said.

"Emergency! Repeat: Emergency! We are coming under heavy air attack and must evacuate. Repeat: heavy helicopter attack. We are going out and must abandon cargo. Can take nothing but radio and small arms. Will contact you when we have a secure base. No time now: must evacuate. Do you read me?"

Albergo thumbed the button and the voice said, not so calm now: "I read you, Happy Dreams. You must wait for instructions. Repeat: You must..."

Albergo switched off.

"Now it's up to them," he said, looking at me. If it went wrong, he'd know who to blame. "We better get ready in case they get here in a hurry. You say they won't. We'll get ready anyway."

The radio was our last link with the outside and we took it out and put it in the strongroom cave before we burned the hut. Sarge carried Albergo's M-16 as well as his combat shotgun. We waited while Albergo unpadlocked a GI locker and Sarge held a canvas sack open while Albergo packed it with stacks of thousand-dollar bills wrapped in plastic. It doesn't take many thousand-dollar bills to make a million. The next locker was full of stacks of hundreds; the third locker contained no money at all: just pure heroin, many pounds of it, worth millions on the street after it was cut.

The money made a lot more weight than the horse; I let that go for the moment. First the chopper, then the rest of it. Kim tried not to show her excitement, but it was in her eyes. Kids are like that on Christmas morning.

"Take it down and put it by the .30 caliber," Albergo told Sarge. "We all know what our positions are.

We had to be ready no matter how long we had to wait. If they didn't come that day, then maybe the day after, or the day after that. The wide flat bare space between the burned-out huts was the logical place for a chopper to land. We were counting on that and positioned ourselves accordingly. Albergo wouldn't be able to do much of anything, so he stayed with the .30 behind a pile of rocks in the shadow of the cliff. I wasn't sure he'd be able to handle the gun when the time came.

We had to be up close when the chopper came down. The pilot and the gunners would be watching the money men as they went up to look in the caves. As soon as we moved in on the chopper, Albergo would cover the money men. That part didn't matter so much; the money men wouldn't be fighters; they hardly ever are.

Sarge crawled under a wrecked jeep, the only cover out there in the open. We got under another. We all had canteens because we might be there for the entire day. There wasn't a sound except for the rippling of the river. It began to get hot.

"Suppose they don't come," Kim said.

"They'll come," I said.

"They may be afraid to come if they think the gunships are still around."

"Gunships can't stay in the air indefinitely. They have to refuel. They have to go back to base. If a raid is successful, they don't do again. This raid was successful. Look around you. You think it doesn't look successful?"

"Albergo may die before they come."

"So what. We don't need him to do this."

"I hope he dies," Kim said.

"We may all die if we don't surprise those gunners. You want to take a nap, take it. You'll wake up quick enough if the chopper comes.

"You take a nap. You're asleep with your eyes open."

I grinned at her. "Let us not go over old business. I told you before. We have a good shot at getting out of here. Hold that thought. Let it suffice for now."

"How can you be so calm?"

"What would you like me to do? Impersonations? Birdcalls? Play the comb with tissue paper?"

Kim moved away as far as she could get. About a foot. Even under a jeep, waiting for the syndicate gunship, I was being cut off, deprived of body contact. Who says women aren't crazy?

You're an idiot, Rainey. How have you managed to stay alive so long?"

"By not listening to people like you."

"Is that what I am to you—people?"

"You are when you try to get me to turn rat. I told you I'm being paid to bring this guy out. I accepted the job, gave my word, got front money. It's a firm assignment and I won't go back on it. And if you can't understand that, think of this. I'm working for a top guy in the Mafia. I'd like not to have to hide in Tibet for the rest of my life."

"He can't be that powerful."

"By himself, he isn't. But he can start the ball rolling. Have you ever heard of an 'open contract?' It means anybody anywhere in the world can hit me and know he'll be paid off. Organized crime isn't a monolithic thing. It's a series of loose alliances. And it works just fine. I don't want it to work on me."

Kim was lying on her side, watching me. "Surely you're not afraid?"

"Just sensible. I always try to be sensible. You should do the same."

"It's too fucking hot under here," Kim said.

I said, "There's the river. Don't let them catch you with your pants down."

Kim yawned. "You make me tired, Rainey," she said.

I didn't think that was true; she feel asleep anyway, clutching the M-16. That was all right; it wasn't set to fire: she couldn't start shooting at something in a nightmare.

It turned out to be a long day; there was nothing to do but lie there and wait for them to come. Albergo was dead, or dying, up in the rocks, his heroin and his money piled up beside him. He might die, but he wouldn't take it with him. Sick as he was, he couldn't stop me from destroying the heroin. But Sarge could, if he got the chance. I would have to do away with Sarge after we took the ship.

The day dragged on like a wounded dog. I ate canned meat and drank water. Kim continued to sleep, muttering in her dreams. Once she cried out, "Squeeze the chocolate!" After that she was quiet for a long time.

It was late afternoon when I heard the chopper. My watch said four-fifteen. Kim opened her eyes though the chopper wasn't close yet. Her face was tight as she pulled the bolt on the M-16.

213

"Rainey, what if they don't land where we expect them to land?"

"We have to do it anyway. No other way out of here. If they open fire, try to make it back behind this thing. Albergo will hit them with the thirty."

"If he's still alive, if he isn't in a coma."

"Then they'll blow us away no matter what cover we have. Look on the bright side. It hasn't happened yet."

The chopper got close and made a pass over the top of the gorge. The big ship sounded like rolling thunder; you could feel its armored menace. It went over and came back, sending shock waves of sound down between the rock walls. Two more passes and it was dropping down all the time.

"They're going to land," Kim whispered.

And so they were. Now the gorge was booming with a great muffled sound. They were coming in slow, but they were coming in. Now they were directly overhead and I could hear shouting coming through the clatter of the rotors. Then the ground shook under us and the rotors whined down to a halt.

No more shouting; two men were talking in Chinese. That went on for a while. I couldn't see the chopper, but I could see the two Chinamen when they started up toward the caves. I nodded to Kim and we pulled ourselves out and crouched behind the jeep. The gunship was right in front of us, no more than fifteen yards away. I could see the pilot, but not the gunners. Both doors were pushed open. The pilot, lighting a cigarette was looking after the two Chinamen, now getting close to where

214

Albergo was. Behind a jeep on the other side of the chopper, Sarge was ready to make his move.

I jumped up and ran. My boots made no sound in the red dirt and I was nearly at the door of the chopper when the pilot saw me. He yelled and threw himself to one side. I saw the startled faces of the gunners. "Hold it," I yelled, but one of them tried to pull a pistol from his belt and I killed him with a short burst. The other guy caught a round that didn't kill him and he screamed and put up his hands. The pilot was out of the chopper, struggling in Sarge's big hands. Up in the rocks, Albergo was yelling. The two Chinamen were standing with their hands on top of their heads. I climbed into the chopper and threw the wounded gunner out of it. He fell on his face and I shot him in the back before he could get up.

I was tossing out the dead man when Albergo opened up on the two Chinamen. They crumpled like rag dolls. He used more lead than he had to; I guess he hated those Chinamen. Sarge had the pilot under control. He picked up the pilot's cap and jammed it on his head.

"Settle down now," Sarge told him. "Ain't nothin' going to happen to you. We need you, boy, so be cool. You be cool now."

No damage had been done to the chopper; it was ready to fly. "Make sure that guy doesn't have a gun," I said to Sarge, who was holding the pilot by the back of his belt.

Sarge scowled at me. "Don't you think I checked? This boy ain't carrying a piece. He's just a flyboy."

215

"That's right," the pilot, a white man, said in an Australian accent. He was thin and wiry and light-haired and not so young. "I just fly these people around. You've got no quarrel with me, mate."

I told him to shut up. Albergo was coming down out of the rocks, gray-faced, limping badly. Kim looked at him, then at me. Albergo staggered but managed to right himself. He had a weird smile on his face. Albergo never smiled, so any smile was weird.

"Very tasty," he said, looking at the gunship. "You know how many times I've looked up at this thing and couldn't get close?"

Sarge let go the pilot and reached up to straighten the shotgun, now slung over his shoulder. I'd seen him do it before. Maybe that's what he was doing now. His hand was just touching the sling when Albergo pulled the forty-five from his back pocket and shot him five times.

Sarge died saying, "Jesus Joe! Jesus Joe!"

His big body folded and fell and lay still. I had the M-16 at my hip, my finger on the trigger. Albergo let the forty-five dangle by his side and I held my fire.

"He was going for the shotgun," Albergo said. "You saw how he was going for it. What's the difference, right?"

I said, "Just don't try it with me."

Albergo looked surprised. "I did it for the rest of us. Why would I try to kill you? We're going out together. You're my bodyguard. It's a long way home."

He keeled over before he could say anything else. His eyes were rolled back in his head;

216

sweat glistened on his face. A long breathy moan came out of him and his chest heaved convulsively. It looked like Joe Junior was not long for this world.

"Get some whisky in him," I told Kim. "Won't do any good. Try it. Put down the rifle. I don't want you getting ideas."

"Let him die. He's dying anyway." She didn't want to shuck the rifle. I was ready to kill her if she started to bring it up. "Rainey, I said let him die."

I had the sixteen pointed squarely at her belly. "Drop the fucking rifle or I'll kill you."

She let the sixteen slide and it fell with a clatter. Then she turned to get the whisky and I could see the USAF .38 in her back pocket. It wouldn't do her any good if she tried to use it. I wouldn't even have to shoot her.

The pilot was standing like a man at a cocktail party full of strangers.

"Can I smoke a cigarette?" he asked, shaking a bit.

"Smoke all you like, mate. Straight answers now. Where do you fly from?"

He got a cigarette going with shaky hands. "From Laos, just over the border."

"And the heroin?"

"It's put on a plane. There's an old airstrip there. The Chinese control it. It's an all-Chinese operation, mate. Look. What are you going to do with me? I'm just a chopper pilot. Give me your promise you won't harm me and I'll fly you any place you like."

"Okay," I said. "You got it. If you don't fuck up."

He blew smoke through his nose, still shaky

but geting a grip on himself.

"Oh, I certainly won't fuck up if I can help it. Have you any destination in mind? Of course, going east is out of the question. We'd have to cross the whole country. We'd be sure to be spotted. Anyway, there's nothing to the east but the South China Sea."

I had been thinking about it. Crazy or not, that's where we were going: the South China Sea.

The Australian was appalled when I told him. "Cripes! What will we do out there? I'm not even sure we have enough fuel to make it."

Kim was back with the whisky and was kneeling beside Albergo. His eyes were open, but he lay like a dead man.

"We're going to land on a ship," I told the Australian. "The South China Sea is full of ships. I don't care what ship as long as it isn't Communist. Don't argue, that's it."

He shrugged and stuck another cigarette in his mouth. "You're the boss, mate. It's better than being dead."

I told him to stay where he was.

"How is he?" I said to Kim.

"You see how he is. You've got eyes, haven't you? It's no use giving him whisky."

"Maybe a ship's doctor can do something for him."

That startled her. "A ship's doctor? What ship?"

I told her what I planned to do.

"It's insane, Rainey." Then she thought for a minute. "Ship from a friendly country, they wouldn't confiscate my share of the money? I *am* going to get a share?"

218

I nodded. "It's not their money. How can they confiscate it? I know nothing about international law. Tell them it's yours and see what happens. They'll probably arrest us, but we'll probably get out of it without going to jail. I'm going to turn over most of the money to the U.S. government. That should buy our way out."

"And the heroin?"

"I'm going to burn it."

This time I got no argument; she had nothing more to say about the heroin. I gathered up the weapons and threw them in the river. I made Kim and the Australian come with me when I burned the heroin. Then we carried down the money sacks and put them in the chopper. Soaked in gasoline, millions of dollars worth of heroin burned bright. Nothing was left but a few wisps of smoke.

"You just destroyed my country's freedom," Kim said, loading the last sack of money.

The Australian understood none of it; he just wanted to get out of there.

"I was thinking of my own country," I said.

It took some doing to get Albergo into the chopper without banging him around; he was only half conscious when we took off, going straight up between the cliffs. The only weapons aboard were Albergo's forty-five, now stuck in my belt, and Kim's USAF revolver. Albergo lay with his head propped against a money sack. Kim still had the bottle of whisky.

It was a big ship and the flight from Laos had been short; the tanks were close to full. We swung up out of the gorge, the pilot got his bearings, and the chopper climbed, heading east.

We went up between the peaks and mist seeped into the chopper, chilling us; moisture beaded on the walls and the windows. Albergo gasped as the chopper went higher and higher. The air was thin, but there was no helping that. If he died, he died.

Then we were through and the mist thinned out and the sky was bright and clear; in the distance was a panorama of lower mountains. The pilot picked up the road to Pleiku and followed it for a while. An hour or so later, Pleiku appeared in the far distance.

"If they have radar down there we've had it," the Australian said. "They'll send bandits to intercept."

But no bandits came and we continued to fly east, going up over the central mountain range that ran north and south through a good part of the country. Here there was more mist and then there was rain. It must have been the rain that kept us from being spotted, or the fact that what we were doing was so audacious. East of Pleiku there were no cities, and that must have helped too.

It got dark and we flew without lights; only the instrument panel was lighted. Kim had been making a few hits on the bottle. She asked me if I wanted a drink. I said no. I looked at Albergo and his breathing was quick and shallow, always a bad sign. If he died, he died. But psychopath or not, I was going to do my best for him. For what it was worth.

No lights showed anywhere in the blackness below us. Up where we were the moon was bright. A big bright tropical moon that looked as if it had been painted on the sky.

"Cripes!" the Australian said. "There's the bloody sea! We made it this far in one piece."

We flew out over the dark waters of the South China Sea. On the white beach were the black shapes of fishing boats drawn up for the night. There must have been a village to go with the boats. No lights showed.

"Fuel's getting low," the Australian called out. "It'll be gone inside of an hour."

"Come down low in fifteen minutes," I told him. "Then we'll start looking for a ship."

Kim took another swig of whisky and cried out, "A ship! My kingdom for a ship! I hate to have to tell you this, Rainey. Albergo just died. Come and see for yourself."

Kim got out of my way and moved over by the door. Albergo was dead all right. I was turning away from the body when I heard the door sliding open. Kim had the .38 in her hand and the hammer was eared back.

"Here's where you get off, Rainey." Her eyes glittered in the half light. "I talked and talked. You wouldn't listen. Too late to listen now. The door is open. You jump out or I'll shoot you."

"Cripes, lady!" the Australian said, stuttering over the words. The chopper began to bounce and slide.

"Jump out, Rainey!" Kim yelled. "I'll shoot you! I mean it!"

She didn't wait for an answer. She pulled the trigger and the pilot let go the controls, frightened out of his wits. Without warning the chopper yawed off to one side and Kim was thrown out through the door, clawing at the frame, screaming, trying to save herself. I grabbed the pilot, shook him, put his hands on the controls. Then his training took over and he brought the chopper up level and steady.

I pushed the door shut and took a drink from the bottle. It lay on its side on the floor and I thought idiotically: square bottles don't roll. Kim was gone to keep company with the sharks. The South China Sea is full of them. Gone—the poor, crazy bitch!

"There's lights down there," the Australian said.

"Take a drink," I said, handing him the bottle. "Get hold of yourself and go down. Put the searchlight on so we can see. If it's a Red ship, take off."

He hit a switch and the big light knifed down through the darkness. It was a big freighter and it rode high in the water. We made a pass and by the time we turned and came back, there were men on deck, all looking up. It took another pass, tighter this time, before we were able to make out the name of the ship."

"The bloody *Canberra*!" the Australian said, jumping out of his skin with excitement. "It's a bloody Australian ship! What bloody luck! It's bloody Australian!"

"Put her down," I said, putting the forty-five on the floor.

We went down into our own glare of light; that big light made everything brighter than noon in the sun. I began to make out the faces of the men on deck. It was crowded now with seamen and officers. They all kept trying to wave us off; they scattered when the downdraft hit them.

222

We touched down on the afterdeck and the Australian switched off the engine. I told him to get down. I got down after him. They came at us from all sides; a tough-looking officer put a heavy revolver in my face.

"You're under arrest, both of you. What the hell do you think you're doing?"

"Trying to get home," I said.

Ten days later I was back in New York, courtesy of the CIA. It took some strong argument before the captain agreed to get a radio message to the U.S.Embassy in Canberra, the Australian capital. Money talks; it talked now. The captain said he'd never seen so much *bloody* money in his life. "Bloody" was just a figure of speech with him. But it really was bloody money.

Albergo's body was refrigerated, pending a coroner's inquest in Sydney, the freighter's destination. I didn't go all the way by sea; a CIA chopper took me off while we were coming up the Australian coast. The money went with me; everything had been fixed at the highest level. The Australians are our friends and they make things easy for Americans. I don't know what happened to the pilot.

The CIA boys questioned me for days. I don't know what they did with the money. But they were glad to see it. I told them everything, even about Kim's resistance movement. They knew about that.

Finally, they let me go.

Before my flight took off for the States, I called Albergo's father and told him his son was dead. I left out a good part of the story, knowing it was buried for good in the Central

Intelligence files.

"He died on the way out," I said. "There was nothing I could have done. There will be a report from the ship's doctor, a coroner's report in Sydney. You can claim the body anytime you like. I did my best for him. But I didn't succeed. You don't have to pay me."

"I'll pay you," he said quietly, "You did all right"

I flew home.